13

Stories

Featuring:

Emilie Collyer
Laurie Steed
George Ivanoff
Blaise van Hecke
Jane Downing
Kirk Marshall
Ryan O'Neill
A.S. Patrić
Louise D'Arcy
Patrick Cullen
Erol Engin
Bel Woods
Les Zig

Foreword by
Peter Farrar

First published by Busybird Publishing 2016

ISBN
Print: 978-0-9953503-2-8
Ebook: 978 0 9873597 7 3

Cover image: Busybird Publishing
Cover design: Busybird Publishing
Layout and typesetting: Robert Frolla
Editor: Robert Frolla
Proofreader: Lauren Magee, Ashleigh Andrews, Sarah Haliem

Busybird Publishing
2/118 Para Road
Montmorency, Victoria
Australia 3094
www.busybird.com.au

Contents

Foreword   i
Peter Farrar

The Other Guy   1
Emilie Collyer

The Punch   11
Laurie Steed

Tall, Dark and Handsome   23
George Ivanoff

The Eleventh Summer   31
Blaise van Hecke

A History of the Kenny Gang   39
Jane Downing

The Artist, at Frankston and Lowe   49
Kirk Marshall

Missing   59
Ryan O'Neill

Movement & Noise   67
   A. S. Patrić

Flat Daddy   75
   Louise D'Arcy

How My Father Dies in the End   83
   Patrick Cullen

The Sea Monkeys   91
   Erol Engin

Get Smart   103
   Bel Woods

Bookstore Fetish   111
   Les Zig

Bios   117

Credits   121

Foreword

Peter Farrar

You have probably experienced it.
While passing someone, you've overheard part of a conversation. Glimpsed something happening from your car window while driving by. You've seen an argument and wondered how it started or how it finished. Or it may have been those two people you overtook while in a hurry, their arms twined together, whispers back and forth barely more audible than breath.

And so it is with short fiction. You don't always have the complete beginning or the neat, fully explained conclusion. You may finish with more questions than what you had on the first page. Short fiction may only be the tip of that iceberg you sense gliding along dangerously under the narrative. It can seem like a preview scene of something bigger. Importantly, whilst short fiction is briefer, it still offers you everything that brings you to a book. To dwell in the writer's sadness, euphoria, love, tragedy, loss and every feeling there is to be experienced through skin and heart.

So, to these thirteen stories that will offer you all this. Look no further than 'The Other Guy' to find a story of lingering regret. Do you want a tuition on what a powerful conclusion looks like? Read 'The Punch' or 'Missing'. How about a vivid sense of place? Then 'The Eleventh Summer' is for you. Truth is, each of these short stories is powerful enough to deserve its own foreword.

Pieces of short fiction these certainly are. But they aren't short on the brilliant writing that is going to make them just as satisfying with a second or third read.

Peter Farrar

The Other Guy

Emilie Collyer

The first thing you told me about yourself was that you worked for MI6. Of course I didn't believe you. Of course, if you really did work for MI6 this would have been the exact result you were seeking.

Do you remember that first weekend we spent together? We met in that flat in South Yarra, the Art Deco one that was down by the river. It was a party and you made a beeline for me as soon as you saw me. I found it very flattering.

We were drinking Stones Green Ginger wine and I was wearing a short Bankusi dress and bare legs and white socks and Doc Martens. They were 8-ups. You wore black jeans and a t-shirt and pointy boots. You were humming a tune as we sat by the river. Hours earlier you had been into the river and you had come up with mud all over your face, like Martin Sheen in *Apocalypse Now*. I knew the tune, I recognised it, but I could not place the song.

'What is it? What's that song?' I asked.

'You know it,' you said. 'Come on.'

I started to hum along and then the words came back to me in a flood. It was a song from the 80s, from my childhood. I sang the words:

'I wo-on't let you down, won't let you down again.'

You laughed. You were delighted with me. You kissed me. I have never kissed a person as much as we kissed. It was heavenly. I never tired of us kissing.

You were living out the back of someone's house in a bay side suburb of Melbourne. You had your own little granny flat. It smelled of incense. You rarely perspired and you had no body odour.

The second thing you told me was that you were a vampire. Now this was back in the days before vampires were everywhere, all over the television and in every book and movie you can throw a stick at.

This was in the days when Lestat from Interview with a Vampire was the go-to-vampire. That was Lestat from Anne Rice's novels, not the Tom Cruise version of him in the movie.

You certainly had sharp teeth, those ones at the sides. I think they are called incisors. And you did used to nip at my neck with your sharp teeth. You had pale skin. You were at least 10 years older than me, but were you 900 years old? You did not wear a cloak and you did not sleep in a coffin. Sometimes you scared me but as far as I was aware, you never sucked my blood.

Subsequently you told me, among other things, that you had turned down a Pulitzer Prize for literature, that you were wanted for a range of political crimes in Pakistan, that you had spent a number of years as a child working for drug lords in Colombia and that you had unofficially broken the world record for free diving.

Then one night, we were at my place, the flat I shared with Helen in St Kilda and we were watching Rage and the song came on. The one you were humming down by the river. I got excited and I sang along. You were already drifting away but you said to me:

'I've got a story to tell you about that song. Remind me to tell you.'

And you fell asleep with my hand curled into yours. And even though my hand went numb I didn't move it because I loved being safe, tucked inside your clasp.

'So what's the story about that music video?'

I asked you this when we were sitting down at the beach. It was cold, a freezing cold winter's day in Melbourne and we were rugged up on the beach, the wind whipping our hair. My hair kept getting in my mouth. I pushed it back behind my ears, time and time again.

'What music video?' you asked me.

'You know,' I said, and I sang the lyrics again, from the chorus.

'A-ha!' You shouted and you jumped and sand went everywhere, all over me, and you were singing, shouting the song into the wind:

'You ask me if I'm happy here, no doubt about it! You ask me if my love is clear, want me to shout it?'

The song is 'I won't let you down'. It was recorded by the band PhD in 1981. The singer was Jim Diamond. There were two video clips made but the one we had seen on Rage and the one most people remember is the one where Jim Diamond is following the girl through the streets and this other guy is following along, trying to sabotage the date. He throws banana peels and drops things from ladders. Ultimately, the three of them end up in a park together and the other guy is playing a piano that sounds like an electric keyboard.

The song has a really, really catchy tune and ever since you had hummed it that night on the banks of the river, it had been in my head a lot.

'So what's the story?' I joined in your mad dancing on the beach and your shouting. 'What's the story?'

You took my hands and you held them in yours. You looked into my eyes and grinned. I had never seen you so happy.

'Well I'm in it of course,' you said. 'I'm the guy,' you said.

'What guy?' I asked.

'THE guy,' you said.

'The guy singing?' I asked.

'Of course not,' you replied and I was relieved. You clearly were not the guy singing. The guy singing was Jim Diamond and you were not him. You kissed me then, softly and with such tenderness and in a flash I wondered if you were going to ask me to marry you. After we kissed, you kept your face close to mine and you touched my face and my neck and my hair with your lips and I was so deliriously happy.

'I'm the other guy,' you whispered into my ear.

'You're my guy!' I said. It was a pretty corny thing to say.

'No,' you said. 'I mean, in the video clip. I'm the other guy. You've seen it. We watched it together, at your place, remember? That's me, the one eating the banana and dropping the bucket of paint and playing the piano in the park at the end.'

I laughed, but you weren't laughing.

The wind was blowing my hair across my face and it was freezing cold.

'What do you mean?' I asked and my voice was shaking, it was so cold.

'What do you mean, what do I mean? I'm the guy,' you said. 'I'm the other guy.'

There weren't many other people on the beach that day. There was a woman walking her dog. She was an older woman and she was dressed sensibly in a red rain jacket and she was wearing a black, woollen beanie. Her dog was a shiny, black, long haired thing with white patches on his face and on his feet.

The woman had an old green tennis ball and she was tossing it into the water and the dog was fetching it and bringing it back to her every time. The ball was getting soggy and wet, from the sea and from the dog's saliva. The woman didn't wipe her hands, she just kept throwing the ball.

You came up behind me and wrapped your arms around me.

'You're like no other woman I've ever known,' you said. I

usually liked it when you said things like that. But on that day it made me feel empty. I didn't want to feel empty, I wanted you to fill me up. I turned around and we kissed. We were forever kissing, do you remember that? It was as if kissing could solve every problem. It nearly could.

And then you disappeared. I went to your place. I looked for you. I asked around. People shrugged and some of them smiled as if that were always going to happen. I didn't go to the police. It didn't seem as though you were missing in a sinister way, you were just gone.

It took me a while to get over you. Then eventually I met a new guy. He was strong and dependable. He didn't believe in vampires or conspiracy theories and thought depression was for people who had too big an idea of themselves. He built cabinets with his hands and the lines were always straight.

I didn't tell him about you. I had stopped looking for you by then, but I had not stopped hoping I would see you again.

The song went around and around in my head. I had only seen the film clip, that one time, late at night. I remembered the tall, leggy blonde and Jim Diamond pursuing her. I couldn't really remember the other guy at all.

I have a son now. There are so many things you don't know about my life. The things we don't know about each other would fill a thousand books, compared to the paltry few things we do know.

My son is ten years old and he is forever on the computer. He didn't directly give me the idea, but one day recently, when I was hanging out the washing the realisation landed. Whole and complete. I could look the song up on YouTube. The song that had been ever elusive, was more than likely now available to me at just the press of a few buttons. I found it easily and I watched it greedily, scouring every inch of the screen for evidence of you.

So this was how I found out that the other guy had a name. He was Tony Hymas. By the look of things, he only did one song with Jim Diamond as PhD. No doubt he hated being referred to as 'the other guy'. No doubt that is how he is often described. He had quite a career before meeting Jim Diamond, and has had an impressive output as a composer and musician since. Many of the titles of his songs and albums are in French.

I looked at photos of him and to be honest I couldn't be 100% sure that they weren't photos of you. It seems like such a strange and specific thing to lie about, that maybe it was the truth after all. Maybe you disappeared because after all the brilliant lies, in that one strange moment of truth, I didn't believe you. Like the boy who cried wolf.

Once, I saw another guy who might be you. He was standing outside a chemist, that one on the corner of Chapel Street and Carlisle Street in East St Kilda. I know that chemist is a methadone clinic. I know a lot more about the world now than I did when we were together.

This guy looked crumpled, like he had just been folded into life, like he was trying to take up as little space as possible. There was something in the slant of his shoulder and the curl of his hair and the little rolly cigarette between his two fingers. And the way he looked up as I walked past, and looked right through me. If it were you, you would have seen me in that moment. You would have smiled.

It's funny how things happen sometimes. We don't use newspapers to wrap fish and chips in any more. Most of us don't even buy newspapers, we read the news online. But the old guy at the op shop wraps things in newspaper. The milk jug that caught my eye and I just had to have.

Is it a coincidence that the page of newspaper he wrapped my jug in contained your death notice? Of course I missed the funeral: A small gathering for close friends. I never thought you were the kind of guy who would have friends put a death notice in the paper, or arrange a 'small gathering'.

I'll admit it hurt my feelings. That's petty isn't it? But there's nothing left to lose now. I can tell you these things. It hurt my feelings that there were people out there who knew you in a way I didn't, who were still in contact with you. And going and dying like that, out of the blue, that's just not fair.

My few memories of us together are so crystal clear and yet I can't remember how you smelled or even, now, what you looked like. All I can recall is the feel of your skin on mine, the clay from the river bed drying on your face, the cold salt air whipping our hair, tangling us up in each other.

I bought some of Tony Hymas's music. It's not nearly as 'poppy' as the PhD song, but parts of it stay with me. A soundtrack to ordinary Tuesdays, hanging out the washing, or just sitting still for a moment, eyes closed, in the afternoon sun.

The Punch

Laurie Steed

I

Rule one is to run until you faint. Run until your breath sounds like a sigh, until the spit hits the road in puddles. Run until your feet kick the pavement and your eyes blur. Run until the exhaust chokes your lungs and you feel as if you are falling.

The contender wanted to win middleweight. He could see himself in the ring, the belt lofted high, every skip, skip, jump that took him closer to his goal.

His father once cut the shoelaces on the contender's sneakers and then challenged the boy to a race. When the boy lost, his father said sometimes life isn't fair.

The contender designed an optimal routine. 6-7: jump rope. 7-8: heavy bag. 9-10: sparring. 10-11 was running, and then back home. He would write 'champion' over and over on a pad in his shed, the roof rattling in the wind like a crowd cheering him on.

He had his son's name tattooed on his ankle and it stung, though not unbearably. The last time he had seen him was when the boy's mother had bundled his son into a car and driven out of the contender's life. He had watched the car getting smaller, his breath making steam in the morning air.

Rule two was to have and to hold, for better or worse, but the contender's wife didn't follow the rules as closely as her husband.

The contender had run in the hope of settling his stomach, but a woman named Kate knocked him down in front of the university. She rode into him, both turning onto the same track. Knocked down by Kate, he had fallen, winded, closed his eyes and waited for the count. Kate thought he was dead, then watched with relief as his chest rose and fell. She dropped her bike and knelt beside him, trying desperately to wake him. After ten seconds he opened his eyes, jumped to his feet, and ran on.

Kate called after him but he kept running. She watched him sprint into the distance, leaves falling off his back as he picked up speed. She noted without sadness that no students had stopped to see if she was okay. She returned to her bike and lifted it from the ground.

Kate walked the bike into uni. She thought of a boy (his name was Aaron, but she avoided saying it for the pain it triggered). It had always seemed like Aaron carried his emotions in a secret compartment: she imagined a satchel in his stomach stuffed with guilt, fear and sadness.

Kate wanted to forget him, as he'd clearly forgotten her, but her emotions didn't care about that. Memories would come and go of their own accord. She studied a cut on her hand and noticed how the palm lines intersected like life's lacerations.

No matter, thought Kate, breathing heavily as she parked her bike. As she turned, she saw a boy, and it wasn't the memory, or the dream, but Aaron, with blood streaming down his cheek from a puffed-up eye socket.

II

Aaron jumped on to the number 19 tram just before it closed its doors. The driver hit the bell twice and Aaron raised his hand in his direction, half-thankful, half-apologetic.

He dropped down into the nearest spot and a Coke can rolled in front of him, paused mid-journey, then kept rolling further down as the tram gained speed. He watched the joggers run laps around Princess Park; he half-heard a Cantonese conversation and a Hindi phone call. He flipped to his study notes. They looked like characters from another language and he wondered when any of it would make sense.

He'd had a croissant and a lukewarm latte for breakfast, hoping it might ignite a greater grasp of post-World War II Europe, but it had failed miserably, leaving him with only the faint aftertaste of smoked ham.

Aaron stared at a man opposite. He was drinking VB from a longneck and swearing at nobody as the tram shook and clattered along the tracks. The man's eyes were like oil stains. He stopped swearing when he saw Aaron staring, and together they noticed the distance between them.

While staring, Aaron thought about his brother Matt, nicotine-stained fingers, passed-out on the couch and Pearl Jam's Alive on repeat. One night, while drunk in the holiday house, Matt had told Aaron a story about a punch. Not just any punch, a particular punch that happened during a basket-brawl in 1977 and left a guy unconscious and lying in a pool of blood.

The unconscious guy hadn't even been in the fight. He had been running to join in, only to have it ended prematurely. When asked about the punch, the guy who'd been hit said he thought a scoreboard had landed on top of him.

Aaron watched the footage days later, saw the brown blood on the parquet, pudding-bowl haircuts and afros tangling with each other while the guy lay on the ground.

Matt was now a full-time drunk, his mail piled up on the front verandah. Aaron worried that he would arrive at work to open the store and Matt would be waiting for a three-pack of longnecks, as if life itself was so unbearable that he needed immediate sedation.

When he was drunk, Matt swayed like he was dancing. He grinned as if he had found his true love, and perhaps he had.

Aaron thought about his own love. She'd seemed so perfect, but one morning he'd woken up lonely and told her it was over.

When he broke up with Kate, he had believed he was doing the right thing, right up until she left his house in tears and he found a knot in his stomach that no drink, distraction or denial would chase away.

Aaron got off the tram. He felt that the only time he ever felt something was when he was saying goodbye.

The leaves shuffled in Aaron's path as he walked towards the university. Aaron turned the corner and had just enough time to see a man, eyes to the ground and running at full pace.

III

After he fell, the contender ran faster.

He licked his knuckle where a scab had reopened, tasted blood, and kept running. The green of the hedges blurred as he ran, and he veered onto a side path into the university.

The contender was keen to study one day. He had grown up with an empty fridge, week after week, and vowed never to live that way as a grown-up. Running on the paths helped him believe that one day, with blood on his lip and a belt around his waist, he would pay off his debts and enrol. Until then, he had a fight to win, and another, and another.

His father had never come close to hitting or holding the contender. His dad was empty bottles by the back door and the sound of the old Holden, coughing and spluttering before getting gone at around 6 a.m. When his father left for the last time he hit the gatepost, and since then it has remained on a permanent lean.

The contender threw shadow jabs as he ran, the sting lingering from a scrape on his elbow. He counted a hundred jabs in quick succession and his father was gone, his wife, gone – the fall, wind kicked out of his lungs – all gone. He figured, not unreasonably, that he could keep punching indefinitely until his thoughts were just energy, jabs, hooks and uppercuts to knock out anyone who stood in his way.

He was nearly at the end of the path when he saw a shadow. He lifted his head in time to see a man – too pretty and his hair too neat – and instead of stopping, barrelled on. Their heads cracked together and both recoiled, and for a moment it was like they were dancing, drunken, and then they fell to the ground.

The contender looked at the other man, barely twenty. He saw fear and he wanted to apologise, but instead, he scrambled to his feet. He ran on, not looking back.

IV

Aaron bet his brother that by twenty-one he would be engaged with a house, a car, and a big screen TV, while Matt would still be jobless and living at home.

Sitting on the warm brick path, he wiped blood onto his hand and licked it clean. He thought of Matt, half-comatose. A hole in the arse of his jeans from where he'd sat on the heater while drunk, red marks burned into his cream-coloured skin.

Aaron never brought up the bet but had been tracking his brother's progress, which for now sat just below the point at which it could be charted.

Aaron felt the collision a second time, his head pulsing, his vision blurred. The impact had felt like a stone cracked hard on his skull. Aaron had wanted to stop the man who had hit him, to tell him he was fine, thank him for the pain he now finally felt.

Two students came to his side and offered to take him to the hospital. At first their voices were just noise, but eventually he heard their words above the ringing in his ears.

He said he was okay, but on standing, fell back to the ground. He said he was okay again, got help standing up, felt the cut on his eye and wiped the blood on his jeans.

They kept talking, both walking in front of him, saying it was okay to need help: he had been hit really hard. Aaron teetered for a moment, paused and closed his eyes, and when he opened them, the students were still in his face, though in truth he could hardly hear them.

V

Kate wished her life was a song to be listened to, felt, and then forgotten at the fade.

She thought about songs that mattered. Most were about loss. She wondered what a song that wasn't about loss would actually sound like, and all she could come up with was 'Jeepers Creepers'.

Aaron made her a mix CD. She still had it, in a drawer beneath a pile of old letters, two watches and a videotape of Chrissie singing 'You're the Voice' on Red Faces.

She thought about tossing everything in the drawer, just emptying out her past until it no longer rattled. When she had listened to Aaron's CD, it had always made her bawl because it meant he'd really cared about her, whatever else she liked to think.

The video of her sister made her cry too, and it occurred to her that these things that were supposed to protect her – to soften harsh edges – these things, these photos and memories, were really just lies on celluloid, someone else's dream from a long time ago.

They had played 'Please Don't Ask Me' at Chrissie's funeral and everyone had cried, though the song wasn't right, or maybe it was – who could tell. Kate figured Chrissie wouldn't have minded, but it wasn't as if she got to ask her.

Aaron told Kate he still believed in her the day they broke up, and she'd wished for a camera at that moment, because for once, it seemed like he had surfaced. By the time she replied, his words had already dissolved like so much sugar.

VI

The contender sat waiting for a tram to take him anywhere else.

He stared at the old hospital from behind its cyclone fence. For a moment he saw faces in the windows. He imagined punching ghosts but they dodged and darted, his fists meeting nothing but air.

The contender thought about the man he had hit, charted the trajectory, the two of them down on the ground but unable to get up, and remembered reading on the gym wall: 'You keep getting up until they fall down.'

He stood up from the bench and tasted blood between his teeth. He realised he could run and run but still their faces would come. His wife would be screaming, the child would be screaming and they'd drive away, again and again, and he could run and run but he would never catch up.

'Are you alright?'

A thin wiry girl with dark hair and glasses was looking at him from a metre away.

'Mm,' he said.

'You don't talk? Are you mute?'

'No.'

'So, are you okay?' said the girl.

'No … not really.'

'I'm sorry.'

'I'll be okay.'

'But you're not at the moment,' she said.

'Are you okay?' said the contender.

'Sometimes.'

The contender laughed. 'Mm,' he said.

The tram pulled up and the girl smiled at him.

'Saved by the bell,' she said, and together they boarded the tram.

VII

Kate watched the blood trickling down Aaron's cheek as he walked towards her. The students who had been following eventually left him alone. Behind Aaron, the library was opening and a bunch of Japanese students had lined up. Kate thought it strange that they would rush in like that, as if learning had its own opening hours.

No matter, she thought, and turned her attention back to Aaron.

She considered approaching him, and would have had he looked genuinely upset, but Aaron looked prouder than usual, entitled. Secretly she wanted to see blood covering his shirt, his jaw misshapen so she could make him better.

Aaron saw her and stopped walking. She took a step towards him, but stopped as he shook his head. He mouthed 'I'm fine' and she wanted to turn and walk away, but something stopped her.

She thought of the man she'd hit on her bike, how he had closed his eyes so quickly when hit. She saw Chrissie slumped against the steering wheel and covered in glass, and she thought of Aaron's face retracting from a punch, his body reeling as he fell to the ground.

'Aaron.'

He turned to her, head down.

She walked closer and when she reached him, wiped the blood away from the side of his lip with her index finger. 'Are you okay?'

VIII

The girl waved to the contender as the tram crossed La Trobe Street.

The contender waved back. He had enjoyed the simplicity of her words, the easy conversation they had shared.

He thought about his wife and the nights when they had stayed up talking, past ten, eleven, twelve, and the traffic noise had died down, their eyes adjusting to the darkness.

He shifted in his seat, not keen to be noticed, knowing that despite the rattle of the tram he would still be heard if thoughts came to tears. Dad says no tears, and it's not an agreement, but a line his father's drawn, as if cleaving his son's parts in favour of the whole.

The contender looked around the tram and it seemed like everyone was in a bubble, white headphones, vacant stares, and the guy who won't get off the phone because they're not listening, and he needs that money, he needs it now.

The cold air from an open window slapped the contender in the face. He pulled with both hands and finally slid the window shut, but the exertion numbed his fingers.

The contender continued to think about his wife. He rubbed his wrist as if wiping away her fingerprints. He thought about another run and rationed that if he ran five kilometres when he got off the tram, he could still make it to work in time to shower, get changed and be on the shop floor by one.

He would miss push-ups and jump rope but he could do that after work. He could jog to the supermarket and come back via the park – a few laps, couple of sprints and home in time for the late news.

He wouldn't pick up the phone because rule three is you don't pick up the phone, don't even think about picking it up, because you only know one number. The person on the end will sound sympathetic but you'll know what they're thinking and no explanation will change that. You have broken one of their rules, which is one of your rules too, but you didn't know you were breaking the rule until afterwards. They will say they want to help, then land a punch that sends you back until the sun has risen and you click, click the kettle until the button glows red.

The contender thought about Tyson. He realised that he never got to tell his son the rules, and that it never bothered him one bit, because his son seemed better without them – unburdened and forgetful.

The contender did not want to leave the tram. He had formed a decision of sorts, to create a different reality, where he called his wife and she listened. He would explain that all he'd ever known was boxing and he knew that didn't make it okay but Christ, he loved her and he loved Tyson, and no one tries to fuck their life up. But memories are a tick, ticking clock and sometimes you feel a knot deep down. You can't get rid of it, not for running or punching or trying to change the way your mind plays the same memory over and over. And you'd stop. But you can't. So you keep running and punching. And it's only when she's hit the ground that you realise you just threw the punch that ended your day, your week, your life.

Tall, Dark and Handsome

George Ivanoff

I was browsing through the paranormal romance section of a quaint little bookstore – you know the sort; quiet, arty and secreted down a side street so that hardly anyone ever finds it – when he bumped into me.

Now, I know this is going to sound like I'm spouting clichés, but he was tall, dark and handsome – honestly, he was. Tall, dark and breathtakingly handsome! And European, I'm sure. Perhaps a hint of the Middle East. He wore an expensive looking suit, the top three buttons of his apricot, form-hugging shirt, unbuttoned.

'I beg your pardon, dear fellow,' was all he said, inclining his head in a slight bow.

His voice was so gentle, yet resonating with inherent power. Confident and self-assured. Obviously a man who got what he wanted. There was a hint of an accent and his pronunciation was too perfect, confirming my assumption of his foreign status.

Our eyes met only briefly, but my knees weakened and I found myself falling into those crystal blue pools. But then he was gone, around the bookshelf and out of my field of vision – perhaps out of my life.

It took me a moment to regain my senses before I realised that I had to talk to this stranger. Had to. Even if my chances with him amounted to a big fat zero – and I knew that they probably would – I could at least hear his voice one more time, perhaps even get him to say my name.

I hurried around to the other side of the shelf, trying to look like I was interested in the books, which, of course, were now the furthest things from my mind.

But he wasn't there.

I surmised that he must have moved further down the shop, towards the beaten up old sofas that people who didn't like paying for books sat in, bending the covers of crappy novels that other people would end up purchasing. I ever so casually raced to the back of the store, peering down the aisles as I went.

Reaching the far wall I was bitterly disappointed to discover a black-clad teenager with way too much make-up halfway through Twilight. I had a momentary urge to rip the book from her grasp and yell at her that it was TRASH, but more important things clamoured for attention in my mind. My mystery man was nowhere to be seen. I went from disappointment to devastation. (Is that too strong a word for this situation? Am I being a drama queen?)

Looking around frantically, I caught a glimpse of him at the front counter, passing a book to the sales assistant, and then another damn book-browser blocked my line of vision. Didn't these people have better things to do than waste their time, and mine, browsing for books in a bookshop?

Hurriedly, without really looking at titles, I grabbed a book from the nearest shelf and rushed up to the counter, accidentally bumping into him, my chest briefly coming into contact with his back, my groin with his firm buttocks. This contact provided much inspiration for my imagination in weeks to come, I can tell you.

'I … I … I'm sorry,' I managed to stammer, stepping back and almost falling over.

'That's quite alright,' he answered, as the elderly lady behind the counter handed him his change and his book. 'No harm done.'

'Ah … so you're a Shakespeare fan,' I blurted out, as I saw his newly acquired book bore the title Much Ado About Nothing.

'That I am,' he answered, smiling warmly. 'And you? What are you reading?'

'Ah …'

I held up The Complete Book of Pregnancy, inwardly screaming as I took in the title. Of all the books I could have picked up, I chose the one mostly likely to give the wrong impression. My man was no longer smiling. Was that a look of disappointment on his face?

'I'm not pregnant,' I blathered. 'Obviously. I mean, I'm a man. And I've certainly not impregnated anyone. I mean … what I'm trying to say is … this book isn't for me. It's … for a friend. A platonic friend.' He raised an eyebrow into a perfect little arch. 'A platonic, pregnant friend … impregnated by someone other than me.'

It was at that point that I wished for the ground to crack open and swallow me. But, of course, it was a vain hope, and in retrospect I'm quite pleased about that.

He looked at me, his smile returning. My handsome stranger. It was not a mocking or deriding smile, as well it might have been. No. It was a kind smile. It was a smile that said, It's okay. I understand. Slowly, he lifted his hand. I'm sure he was about to touch me. It was all like a diffused moment in a soppy film.

But then the woman behind the counter cleared her throat noisily, destroying the moment.

'What?' I demanded, snapping around to glare at her.

'That will be twenty-seven dollars and ninety-nine cents.' And she sneered at me. That's right, the bitch actually sneered. It was like she was trying on her Billy Idol impression. I wanted to tell the old bat that I didn't really want the fucking book (that, and that it was way too late for her white wedding), but he was watching me and I didn't want to appear any more foolish than I already had. So I handed her the book, smiled tightly, and started to rummage through my manbag. (Don't you just HATE that term, 'manbag'? I mean, who came up with that? But, what else can you call it?) Finally finding it, I pulled out my credit card and triumphantly waved it under the woman's nose.

She made a sniffling sound, which I'm certain was meant to be rude, and took the card delicately between the tips of her wrinkly old thumb and forefinger, as if it was loaded with diseases rather than money that didn't belong to me. As she processed the purchase, I turned to discover that my stranger was gone.

Again.

'Sign here,' said the woman, sliding the receipt and a pen

across the counter to me, whisking her hands away quickly so as not to be in danger of accidently being touched by me. She then carefully placed the credit card on the counter, signature facing her, ready to compare it to the receipt, eager to scrutinise.

I stared at her for a moment, her face lined with despair and age and heaven knows what else, and then snatched my card up. Heading for the door, I called over my shoulder, 'I've changed my mind. You read the book. Tick, fucking tick!'

Outside, I looked along the street just in time to see him walk into another store. Hurrying after him, in as casual a way as I could manage, I peered into the window of a tobacconist. My stranger stood by the cash register exchanging words with a hunched, bearded, hobbit-like man who looked like he had just walked off the set of a Lord of the Rings film. Tall, Dark and Handsome towered over Short, Pasty and Ugly, reached into his pocket and pulled out a pipe.

A pipe? I thought. Yes, very suitable for my mystery man. I immediately had a vision of the two of us in front of an open fire, him, dressed in a smoking jacket, leaning against the mantel, puffing on his pipe and reciting Shakespeare as he blew smoke hearts towards me. Yes, I know, smoke hearts are probably impossible, but hey, it's my vision, okay!

I watched as he handed the pipe to the hobbit, cautiously. His gaze darted from side to side, as if he were expecting to be watched, and then met mine. I gasped. His eyes widened. It was an ever so brief ocular union, from which I extracted myself promptly. I pulled away from the glass and darted into the café next door. I didn't want him to think that I was some sort of crazed stalker. Because, I'm not!

I strolled the length of the café, the eyes of the waitress following me, waiting for me to pick a seat. I didn't sit down. I picked a menu from an empty table and pretended to examine it. After a couple of minutes, I tossed the menu back onto the table and headed outside, the waitress glaring at me as I left.

He was escaping. The object of my desires and fantasies was rushing down the street, turning a corner, and making haste out of my life before he had had a chance to really enter it.

By the time I got to the corner, he was long gone. He had disappeared without a trace, like some counter-espionage double-agent.

I wandered back past the tobacconist, despondent until I spotted a leather tobacco pouch on the path. I picked it up, tentatively pulled back the flap and sniffed, imagining that it was his, images of what could have been tantalising my mind's eye. The sweet scent of the tobacco filled my nostrils and my imagination.

A black corvette drove past, the window down. Was that him in the driver's seat? I almost flagged down a taxi, intending to demand that the driver 'follow that car', but thought better of it. I mean, that would have been going just a little too far.

Instead, I inhaled again. Who was he really? An infamous spy with an international reputation? A master criminal on the run from the law? The crown prince of some small but wealthy country that no one had ever heard of? Maybe a high-priced gigolo, used to fulfilling the fantasies of aged widows with bucket-loads of their dead husbands' money, who occasionally jumped the fence to taste greener grass? Endless possibilities.

Or perhaps he was just an ordinary man? Merely a receptacle for my wildly improbable hopes and dreams?

One last sniff and I closed the pouch, safely tucking it away into my pocket.

No, I shook my head with certainly – definitely not ordinary.

The Eleventh Summer

Blaise van Hecke

Wild children are dancing with the waves by the deserted beach; the sun catching the tops of their heads as they bob in the foamy bath. Nearby, other children clamour over the rocks prying oysters from their sleepy lives, chucking them into a bucket already brimming with grey gnarly shells. With the bucket tipping and swaying, the children skip and holler back to camp.

Hey, guys, come get some. Quick.

Yeah, hurry or we'll eat 'em all up.

The camp sprawls out below salty trees and washing flaps in a stiff breeze. The fire splutters and pops as the billy burps with boiling water. A log, serving as the kitchen seat, holds one small child still in nappies, his tummy out of proportion to his skinny limbs, his hair crazy from the wind, the sand, and the salt. Surrounding him is a haphazard

31

group of ancient army tents, groaning with age. The wave riders come racing up the beach full of bravado, whistling and shrieking with mammoth tales of daring.

Four brothers clamour for a spot on the kitchen log. Lined up they looked like Russian dolls; smaller versions of each other with squinting eyes. None has seen a brush or bath or a pair of shoes in a good while – hair taking on a life of its own. Everyone claims extreme fainting hunger, the competition escalating.

The oysters are spirited from their shells, hardly seeing the light of day as they are slurped from their homes into the mouths of squawking baby birds. The faithful Labrador waits patiently for pass outs, which don't appear, except from the one in nappies. With food in their bellies, the boys challenge each other and are off over the sand dunes, their voices trailing in the wind, the dog hot at their heels, the one in nappies toddling in their wake.

Suzy does love the boys but sometimes they give her the shits, laughing at her when she has sand in her bum crack. The boys are good value but noisy; the oldest is Rolly (a bit older than Suzy), then Billy, then Vincent, then little Johnnie (still in nappies). Then there are Suzy's little brothers: Billy and Jack.

The second syllable of Suzy's name is snatched by the wind and buried in the sand. She takes little notice of the boys as they wave and shout a half-coherent story at her from the rocks. She is busy with her plaits. Suzy wanders around the campsite holding tightly to one finished plait, looking for a tie. She finds Johnnie, dad to the boys, squinting into the camp oven, his eyes water as he tries to shield them from the smoke.

'Hey, Johnnie, do you have a lacker band?'

'Eh?'

The father of four boys looks at the girl with one plait and dimples as if she is an alien. He rummages through tin plates, muttering to himself.

'There you are, little miss ... pig-tails.'

'Thanks, Johnnie, hey, they're plaits ya know.'

'Hmm ... oh, okay, miss ... plaits.'

He retrieves his bread from the fire, swearing at the hissing billy teetering over the flames.

The lacker band does the job although it pulls a couple of hairs and makes her eyes sting. Rubbing them makes it worse, on account of the salt and sand. She hangs around long enough to see a blue kombi pull up and a family tumble out. She doesn't linger, since there are babies, and they are bad news because before you know it, you are stuck looking after them. Then, you have to listen to adult conversation. She's heard all the stories a trillion times plus infinity. She picks up a piece of Johnnie's warm fresh bread, dips it in honey, and races over the sand, which grates her toes but feels good.

Suzy undresses on the bank and swims the inlet, heading for the rocks, the choppy water frothing around her ears. She imagines herself a beautiful mermaid, with her hair in long plaits, adorned with a garland of seaweed – until she remembers that there are eels in the water. The boys are impressed that she no longer needs the rubber tube to help her cross, like last summer.

Come on Suze, hurry up.

Come see these giant crabs, they're real fast.

Fast as lightning.

They're grouse and real snappy.

Rolly and Billy cackle with glee, their naked sunkissed

bodies clamouring over the rocks, all monkey limbs, poking and prodding at nooks and crannies.

The novelty of crabs wears off when they have managed to scare them all into hiding, so they sit on the rough rocks, the spiky bits sticking to their bum cheeks, with their feet in the little warm pools of water, nudging at periwinkles with their toes. The oyster bucket remains empty, and only the promise of food gets them back across the inlet, to the camp, when so many grown-ups are around.

By the late afternoon, the camp has swelled with people as they set up more tents. The whole place is warming up to it: the dance at Murrah Hall. Kids are running everywhere and you can't really tell who belongs to whom. Before they know it, they are getting their faces washed and their hair smoothed with little lasting effect. Suzy's mum even finds her a skirt. It's made from red woven hemp and has blue flowers embroidered on it. She unplaits her hair and rather likes how it has gone kinky, like the waves.

Later, at the hall, the band is setting up. Matty is tuning his guitar, while he holds a cigarette with his teeth, twang, twang, twang … Margo, the back-up singer, is counting into the microphone, one two, one two …

Children duck and weave through the crowd. Before long, the music is turned up. Up to Suzy's earlobes and out through her hair. She is in heaven. She dances, she jigs, she rocks and she waves. She makes her skirt billow out around her knees and she dances with Rolly until her bare feet hurt. While the moon cruises across the sky, Suzy enjoys the first dance that she has ever noticed.

'Hey, Suze, look at this.'

She gazes into the eyes of her grinning, stomping partner and feels strange feelings like never before. The moon is high and Suzy feels even higher, from the beating of her feet on the wooden planks to the twirling and the whizzing of her new skirt.

It is strange when the band stops for set break and a drink at the bar. She can't stop the buzzing feeling at the end of her toes and her fingertips and even along her hair, which seems even kinkier than she remembers. Suzy goes outside to find her brothers – wondering if they too are full to their eyeballs with this feeling.

Tommie, from the band, is sitting on the back steps rolling a cigarette. He shifts his weight onto his elbows to lean back and look at the sky. The missing brothers are now forgotten as Suzy skips towards Tommie – who she secretly wants to marry – and she is smiling from ear to ear. All the kids think that Tommie is IT. He is old enough to drink and smoke and drive a car, but he will still talk to them as though they are real people, rather than little kids. Suzy runs up the steps and plonks down next to Tommie and pulls her knees up to her chin and wraps her arms around them. This is mostly to still her jigging muscles that are still dancing.

'There's my Suzy girl. How are ya, mate?'

Tommie grins and puts his arm around her. This makes her tilt her blond head towards him. She is still bursting with this newfound love of the music. She can smell the tobacco smoke in his clothes and a hint of beer on his breath. She closes her eyes to the world in an effort to trap it all, but the darkness makes her a little dizzy.

'How's that music, Suze? Gets the place really jumpin', doesn't it?'

Tommie's deep velvety voice is mesmerising, but she can barely hear what he is saying above other voices and the music still echoing in her head, so she remains with her head on his shoulder, eyes closed, and sighs.

'Do ya like it, Suze?'

'Yeah, Tommie, I really really love it. You're a great bass player.'

'Thanks, princess; it's all I live for.'

'It's like a whole other planet.'

Tommie laughs in agreement and they are silent.

'Hey, Suze, have you ever kissed someone?'

'Course I have, Tommie, I kiss me brothers and mum and everyone else, all the time.'

'No, Suze, I mean kissed like a grown up?'

'Nah, I'm not a grown up.'

'You are, just 'bout.'

'Hmm …'

Her eyes close.

Then she feels something warm near her ear and shrugs it away before realising that someone is kissing her neck. Suddenly, all the wild and wonderful feelings turn to a strange spasm in her guts, under her belly button, and even though she doesn't know why, she knows she no longer wants to marry Tommie. She is sure she doesn't even like him now that she is centimetres away from his face that has a strange look to it. This reacts to that feeling in the guts, which must be that thing that Mum was talking about, called gut feeling or intuition. Funny how you don't know the real meaning of a word 'til it's looking at you. Next, he puts his wet tongue in her ear. This sends her knee into his chin with a thwacking sound and she isn't sure, but maybe he bites his tongue 'cos he swears real loudly.

Just as Suzy runs headlong into Rolly in the hall, the music comes booming out of the amps, and he swoops for her hands before she can argue and takes her back to her dizzy self. His hair stands out all around his head like a crazy halo, and his stomping rhythm seems all out of kilter, but the beam on his face is like a beacon. She is so happy that she feels like she is flying across the sky with the moon and the stars. She flies and flies until her legs become numb.

As the moon makes its slow descent into the trees, the party slows down and becomes a low hum of worn out revellers. Suzy, Rolly and the rest of the boys then pile in with the other kids, no longer caring that there are babies, who are sleeping soundly in the jumbled interior of the blue kombi van.

Suzy dreams of beautiful mermaids dancing in the waves, wearing periwinkles in their blond hair, which radiates from their heads like rays of moonlight. They throw back their heads and laugh at length, exposing pale throats. The stars glitter on the surface of the water, winking at her in a knowing way, as the mermaids take to the inlet and race each other to the rocks and back until they lay exhausted on the sand. They sit up suddenly when they hear voices approaching and grow human legs that carry them swiftly across the sand dunes and out of sight, leaving a trail of faint giggles and the soft splashing sounds as they return to the depths of the sea.

A History of
the Kenny Gang

Jane Downing

It's mostly bills: electricity, gas, Telstra. They can sit in the letterbox for days and there's evidence they go unopened even when they're taken in. On late afternoons near-abouts the winter solstice their house will be the only one in the street without the warm glow of electric light. No lights, no heating: the curtains in the front room crawl with mould.

You can tell a lot about people by what they get in their mail, though not as much as in the past; the intimacy of the internet has taken a lot off the streets. I've been delivering down Mansfield Street for years and at their place I also drop the letters from the Parole Board and Centrelink. But there's never been a postcard or a foreign stamp or an enveloped letter without the tell-tale plastic window.

They can't have had an easy life to end up on Mansfield Street. It's the rough end of a rough town, outside the outskirts, where red brick has well and truly given way to weatherboard and fibro. The indestructible crepe myrtles are dead. I weave my sturdy red postie's bike between the carcasses of clapped out cars and the guts of washing machines to get to a letterbox that was once painted an identical gay red. The parody is chipped down to the metal now.

I heard rumours about the family whose names appeared in those rectangular plastic windows. This is a small place, it'd be impossible not to. With marriages and shacking-up and step- and half- they were collectively the Kennys. When the most famous son hit the city papers there were more facts: a mother with too many children, a father dead, step-father as young as he was. You really can't tell anything from such outlines. These were cartoon people without the colouring in. Without movement. But you might consider some of the details part of mitigating circumstances if you're so inclined.

Eddie Kenny was twenty-five when it was all over.

There's always a different car or two or three flattening the weeds in the gravel drive. Evidence of drug dealing or theft: Eddie was charged with both at an early age.

There was one early interview when he looked rakish with black, straight eyebrows like artist's charcoal above glowing eyes and designer stubble which no doubt owed more to dodgy hygiene than an eye for the fashion pages. To this journalist he explained the car thefts away with a pithy line: 'they were only a borrow – a man has to get from A to B.'

It didn't make him an instant celebrity but it didn't do any harm. Who in this world isn't looking for a way to get from one place to another?

The marijuana in the backyard was, if anything, easier to pass over. Even his mum had been up before the magistrate for drug possession and supply. The received wisdom in this day and age is that the laws are the problem not the dealers. The shootings were not so easily dismissed.

I saw it on the tv. The police had some warrants out and Eddie'd gone to ground in the bush across the range from Mansfield Street – kangaroo and wombat territory not yet overrun by tree-changers. Who can tell what really happened? Eddie and his mates moved on to major crime after that and three coppers got State funerals. We all knew about police corruption but the widows' faces on the 6 o'clock news gave you pause.

For a while it was difficult getting to the Mansfield Street letterbox because of the media camped on the footpath. Then there was another bit of human interest elsewhere with a photogenic face and things slipped back to normal: more bills, probation meeting reminders for sundry family members, a newsletter from the sitting MP which slowly mulched at the base of the box.

Being in the pub the night they took hostages was, like most things in life, chance.

The town has one primary school, one independent supermarket, a hardware and a railway station where no trains stop. No bank, no pharmacy, no doctor's surgery. No post office. I collect my letter-stuffed satchels from the town closer to the highway, that great artery that saps the lifeblood from the diabetic flesh of the north-east. But of course we have two watering holes, both clinging onto dignity. No shoes, no shirt, no service.

My cousin suggested the top pub that night. The tv was on the blink so I stayed on past the normal couple of pots. I knew most of the crowd in the one room exemplar of the rural hotel, by sight, by correspondence. Ten or twelve of us in all. I didn't recognise Eddie Kenny when he walked in flanked by his mates. They'd cleaned up to come out of hiding. They all wore the jeans and flanno uniform of the dispossessed, but washed new with crisp lines along the rumples and creases.

I did see each dump a duffel bag against the front wall on their way to the bar. The pile of black and blue canvas stamped with sporting logos attracted a little bit of attention, but didn't look like an intention to terrorism. This was Australia, not the London Underground, New York's JFK or LaGuardia.

I was talking to my cousin and only tuned in when a voice too loud for this place asked for whiskey. Not beer? Of course I turned. Three blokes were in the far corner, and one was at the bar doing the asking. Katey, twenty-something, hair stylist, member of the Michael Jackson fan club and subscriber to Vanity Fair, shuffled closer along the worn edge of the bar and asked, 'You're Eddie Kenny aren't you? You were at school with my sister.'

She sounded flirty. The town didn't have much – indeed anything – to offer. No doubt she subscribed to more than one internet dating site as well.

From where I was standing there was no cause and effect in anything that came next. They were, this gang, if not already drunk, on something harder, nastier. I suppose if Eddie and his mates had been entirely rational in the coming hours, that wouldn't have made sense either.

'Okay, that's it,' Eddie was shouting. 'Lock it down boys.'

The publican, name in flaky gold above the door, protested as Eddie's mates jumped from their slouches and shot the metal bolts up into the lintel and down into the worn groove in the cement. The guns came out of the duffel bags and he shut up. They were not the sawn-off shotguns they describe in your traditional bank raid; we were in the country here and they swung full tilt rifles over their shoulders, cradled them like babies in their arms. Two barrels each, like pig snouts.

Our fear lit up the place like it was a stage. Suddenly we were all acting.

'We're not going to hurt you,' Eddie Kenny said. He held one of the rifles, shiny with years of palm oil sweated along the barrel. He said it again, louder. He had a voice as smooth as a nineteenth-century pew. I almost believed him about the hurting. My cousin pulled us into the seats of the closest table, making us smaller targets.

Then we had to hang onto our fear and watch the show.

The weaselly mate and the stouter one took up positions on each side of the front door, resting against the wall, the tips of their firearms etched black against the light coming off the street lights and through the twin windows.

The one we came to know as Eddie's little brother went around collecting our mobile phones. He wouldn't believe Karl – Farmers' Federation, Victoria's Secret catalogue for his wife, fat letters from their son in Japan – didn't have one. Karl plopped peppermints, a wallet and an improbable length of twine – in the manner of a twelve year old boy –

on the bar. Eddie's brother obeyed when Eddie said, 'Leave it,' and we all hoped Karl was bluffing and had help, any help, on speed dial in his other pocket.

The silence palled. Eddie was pacing to the windows, back to his brother, now behind the bar spewing the whiskey into schooner glasses. Eddie was a caged lion and we were locked in the enclosure with him.

Much has been written about the stories he told, and more about the way he told them during the siege. He had a pretty turn of phrase. He was even singing at the end. I didn't recognise the lyrics. Maybe he made them up: they were about the world being all wrong. His songs were a fitting chorus to the complaints.

They'd never had a chance according to the script. The powers-that-be were against the rural poor, they looked after their mates. We'd be 'fools to bother about parliament,' he said. He had a captive audience in every way. We all knew life was easier in the cities. We'd complained about it often enough ourselves, about the faceless men with deep pockets. But we were used to mumbling it into our beer not punctuating every sentence with a rifle butt against a table top.

The general malaise he kept banging on about then evolved into specifics. Seems there were once five mates in Eddie's gang. One lay out there, beyond the bolted door, cold and getting colder. He'd dobbed them in, a rat in the ranks, a sneaking snake in the grass, a traitor. He'd deserved it. We've all been deceived at one time or another, so you know what sympathy he had to draw on in his audience.

Eddie went around the tables while he told his stories, dispensing the whiskey with his wisdom. He winked at me, like he knew me. I was flattered. A man who'd made the front pages of the city newspaper recognised me. He turned to my cousin, sloshed the alcohol, and winked at him too.

He told us their hideout was blown thanks to the traitor. His hand was forced. He had no choice. It sounded like he was teaching the party line as much as he was entertaining his spontaneous party. Too many westerns on Saturday afternoon telly shaped his language. He used the phrase: Last stand.

Before the stand, before the singing, was the dancing. Flirty Katey had made herself small but Trude wanted to go home.

'I have the babies in bed. I have to be back when they wake,' she pleaded. Trude was once a pretty little thing photographed in the regional paper dancing at the eisteddfod. Ballet. Leaping off the ground, no strings attached. Two de factos and three sons later she was worn completely thin.

Maybe Eddie remembered the eisteddfod photo too.

'Not yet sweetheart, it's time to dance,' he told her.

Eddie's brother tipped a coin into the jukebox near the toilet door. Made a choice. Punched in his selection. Eddie put one hand in the small of Trude's back, took her hand in his other. If she'd been a couple of foot taller, they would have been cheek-to-cheek.

I saw her face as she was swirled past. One eye staring out from armpit height, the other buried in his smell. The tension across her shoulders was so tight you could trampoline off it and hit the ceiling.

I had to look away. The backlit Galliano, Crème de

Menthe, the Blue Curacao and flowery liqueurs on the top shelf behind the bar looked like an old stained glass window on a hopeful Sunday.

The toe-tapping rhythm of Scissor Sisters' 'I don't feel like dancing' drowned out the stories for a while. Eddie's brother moved morosely to the window with the weaselly one.

In cities any short, sharp percussive noise is written off as a firecracker or backfiring car. Rifle fire isn't so easily discounted. It sounds deeper. The shots have more resonance. Meaning.

The weaselly mate stopped rubbing his nostrils across his sleeve long enough to take the first shot. Until that moment the pub had been bombarded only with loud speaker demands. The police turned up without a call from Karl's non-existent mobile. It was only a matter of time, once they found their informant's – or in Eddie's parlance, the rat's – body. They'd checked the other pub first. Then there was us.

Clichés survive because they slip off the tongue so easily. I lay on the spongy, rotting carpet thinking: a hail of bullets. Glass shattered, my stained glass window exploded behind the bar. To this day there's a hole in the side of the bar you can stick your little finger in. The cash-register ching of the cock and fall of shells were drowned under the screaming that flew across the scale, Katey's high C to Mr Forrest's wounded bull.

'It's us against them.' 'We'll never surrender.' 'Fucking mongrel coppers never gave us a chance.' Eddie strung out his pearls until the stouter of his mates slipped and staggered into the frame of the right-hand window. To the police marksmen outside he must have looked as stark a target as a metal rabbit in a sideshow shooting gallery. Which of the thunder of booming bullets took him out was impossible to say. It was as if he was throwing himself backwards. Once he was on the ground, at my level, down there, I could see the blood pooling across his blue and brown flannaletted-chest.

Eddie's brother was sitting at the bar, his back to the fight. He had that look about him – an emaciated sheep standing in a dirt-dry paddock. This was his last stand. Maybe I could have jumped up and stopped him. I watched as he stretched his arms full-length and tilted his neck back so he could prop his rifle in his mouth.

The weaselly one left at the window must have been watching too. Is suicide contagious like yawning? His brains stuck to the inside of the window like a thrown omelette.

Eddie Kenny didn't pause. He unbolted the pub door and marched out, rifle loaded with two shells. Bravado his only armour.

Two of the pub's patrons also died that night. Martin Cherry and Jack Jones were their names. Jack was my cousin.

A lot has been written since that night of the killer who charmed the pub with his stories and swept the women up in dance. I'm told there's talk about a television documentary on real crime, a novel or two.

Eddie Kenny is in jail. We don't hang our criminals

anymore. He'll be receiving fan mail and the usual letters lifers get from dysfunctional women proposing marriage. I still see Trude's dazed eyes as she swirled past our table.

She doesn't live in town anymore. But I still deliver to the Kenny place. There's a pink tricycle and a rusty scooter in the front yard most days: a new generation with grudges.

I take Jack's kids to Maccas on the highway on Saturdays to give their mum a break, as much as them a treat. And I tell them what a top dad they had. Which is the truth.

The rest are just stories. There'll be more, writing and rewriting, and I don't claim much. This is just one history.

The Artist, at Frankston and Lowe

Kirk Marshall

He first moved into our neighbourhood that year, before our streets were stricken by the terrific winter-propelled winds of March. Not many of us could brave the scorn of the collective in claiming to understand why he'd chosen our insipid mid-western borough as the geographical quarter from which to produce his valued work. Nor could any one of us comprehend, if we were beyond contempt to make a grave peace with our failings, why it was us that he chose to adopt as his new suburban family; but many of us were less than culturally refined, quite a preponderance of us were obscenely fearful of the powerful sincerity of any external force beyond our hedgerow-bounded hamlet, and most of us were busy burying ourselves deep into the throes of a mid-life hibernation of faded ambition, self-loathing and trebled mortgage repayments to consider the threat an artist might bear upon our honourable, horrible little estate. We could not encompass with any genuine exchange of foresight or canny insight, how his arrival might inform the trajectories of our later lives. We preferred not to think; we consoled ourselves by demonstrating that we were above speculation. His name was Luke Quinn O'Florin, a precocious and well-travelled twenty-six year-old watercolourist from a stock of Irish confectionary merchants, a starry pupil of the Sorbonne and the tutelage of Rothko, someone whom contrived a world of shape and colour from the grim stasis of the everyday. When we afford the time to look back, now, and interrogate the changes which Quinn influenced upon our common existence, we often wonder over what shape he each allocated to us, what hue he surmised was applicable to the movements of our dreams and lies.

There was one woman whom we all treasured and adored, because it was she whom had set the compass of our desires on divining our perfect counterpart, attuned the astrolabe of our each wanting heart upon the implacable sea of eligible partnership. We all liked to believe we were deserving enough to bed Soleil Belize, because such a confidence emboldened our own marriages and romantic fripperies; and because it was she whom had inspired within us an understanding of the glamour of sex and unity, we each conspired to win her affection so as to feel included within her appreciation of all things bodily impassioned. Soleil was quick and gallant with Spanish blood, and on Tuesday afternoons in our borough, before our children returned from school to bemoan to us the education system which we championed and cavorted sentimental over, she would pry open the shuttered window-blinds of her second-story bedsit, and come trouncing down the external stairs in her berserk one-piece bikini, the wide and obscene and joyous contour of her pelvis swinging like a barometer as the mercury in our loins soared to all-time summer highs and the backs of our knees itched in such a way that only the tapered Day-Glo pink of our neighbourly priestess's acrylic nails would satisfactorily be able to reach. We were fond to trade awful gestures attesting to our manhood, deludingly provide fanfare at the way the florid elastic appeared to ride up her outer thigh as she descended, offer ineffectual wolf-whistles and exercise heartless leers like we were the quarterbacks of '68 assembling for a victory photo. But we all knew we'd never share the linen strewn about Soleil's high-ceilinged studio, or taste the sordid European mouth through which she daily pressed carnations against the surface of her tongue. We were all old men, and our youth and stamina were long but starved of patronage and gratitude, and much of our hair was falling out whilst we showered, and many of us had abandoned the passtime of moonlit masturbation due to early mornings and workaday inconvenience. Soleil Belize constituted the arbiter and bombshell star for our arid weekly theatre, and not once did she reprimand us for our travesty of communal surveillance; more than this, she downright invited our spectatorship, and like a sport we longed to play but forever were ill-equipped to try out for, we'd pass each other frosted bottles of ginger ale and crowd around our stoops and lawnmowers like a committee of strays with testicles paraded high, and we'd allow her to dalliance in the rubber ring-pool inflated at the front garden of the apartment complex, her hair slick with water.

'Look smoking today, Ms. Belize!' we'd insist, rolling up the cuffs of our sleeves.

'That pool's awful kind to cool you down, Soleil,' we'd venture, wheeling out our barbecues.

'Local newscast's cautioned against single women spending time alone in dwindling light,' we'd bark, as the sun consumed all.

The objective of our courtship was not to convince her of our desirability, our worth; then and only then would our plan irrevocably come undone. Ours was a direct defiance of all that which littered our individual histories, evidence exemplifying our superior ordinariness. This is why, when Luke Quinn O'Florin shook the foundations of Soleil Belize's unwinnable heart, and ascended the external stairwell after returning her home following a spring night's dinner-dating, his hand interlinked in her own, that our campaign lost its elegance, our dream was corrupted and our plight diminished. We never did forgive Soleil Belize for abandoning us all in such a way; we agreed on good authority that this represented just another example of how our legendary mettle and uniqueness were squandered on someone wholly uninspired and unseeing. We resumed wearing shirts with sleeves, we sold our barbecues, we hid the Ferris Bueller sunglasses we'd persisted in hounding our wives for. We consorted to extinguish our memories of Soleil in her swimsuit the full spectrum of the Amazon greenhouse. We sought comfort in knowing that Quinn only truly wanted her for her aesthetic prowess; and as is the nature of all artists, someday soon he would forsake her as he would a particularly impulsive canvas. Then, only then, would we gloat and bray and reapply hair product, for the day when a heartbroke Soleil would resurrect the spectacle of her public afternoon bath. Only then would we come to feel like our solidarity was accepted as some kind of love.

The wedding was hosted in the chapel on Levinson Ct., where the larches bowed to the ground and carpeted the sidewalks with dying crimson foliage. We'd received invites inscribed on elaborate gold letterhead in our mail shoots, the sort of card-stock we might once have associated with corporate professionalism and the personalised cover letters of committed youngblood, but which we now came to intimate with betrayal and desertion. Soleil Belize was to be escorted by her pensive restaurateur father with cheeks scored by butterfly rash, and Quinn was to be bookended by his eight brothers, a quandary of faces and voices borne of clover and stout, a collusion of hoarse Irish wharf-speak which we neither grasped nor edified, save for imitation during quiet moments in the toilet behind the vestibule, whenever a sister of Soleil sauntered passed. The celebrant was a Reverend Allbright, purloined from a diocese over, to perform the rites and hallowed ceremonies of matrimony, but he looked half-blind to us, and possibly even lecherous, as we presided over the slap-dash chaos of this thrown-together marriage shambles, and we prided ourselves over our poisonous words whilst we devoured the spread and downed liquor at the punch-table. Quinn traded vows with Soleil, prematurely announcing her as his 'most adored example of modern art', and Soleil's father wept lovingly without consolation into the suit-sweetened shoulder of one of Quinn O'Florin's brothers, who promptly slapped him on the back and addressed him as 'Dad'. The flower girl threw a shoe down the aisle, before being industriously bustled toward the front of the altar, and the best man expressed emotions of mock disbelief to those members of the greater Belize family immediately seated beneath the canopy of the fibreglass-and-plaster crucifix, as the reverend interpreted verses from St. Paul to the sinners of Absalom.

When the vast doors were thrust wide, eliciting the awed chorus of canoodling prom royalty and the rapid-fire cannonade of trigger-happy flashbulbs, we queued in a procession of false modesty and herringbone uniformity, rubbing the toes of our suit heels into the backs of our pants' legs, straightening the newly-cultivated carnation blossoms pinned at the splay of our lapels. We wracked our dormant arsenal of untarnished sentiment for an appropriately-dispatched type of well-wishing, we plumbed whole leagues into the depths of our unfamed childhoods to remember what our own fathers had offered us upon getting hitched, and worked to regurgitate it to Quinn and Soleil as though we were the rightful authors. These were the glory days, we'd whisper, knowingly; the sex would only improve once, after this, in his life – and that would be after she'd fallen pregnant and invested her days affecting exotic forms of aerobics, we boasted, conspiratorially; she should never doubt his tenacity and strength as a friend, as well as a lover, we protested; they would make such a predetermined coupling, that one day within the imminent future – we informed their parents – it would be as though they were born beneath the same Irish (or Spanish) roof. We each presented Quinn and Soleil with our waffle-toasters, and complete set of Britannica business planners, and nine-irons and twenty-piece spork sets, respectively; then we gazed with unenviable disdain as the beautiful pair careened away in their half-hour limousine rental to a honeymoon future in some place unimagined and mythopoeic (maybe Toronto, perhaps Wales). We filed out in a studious humility, marshalling our children and wives across the asphalt and down the narrow lane between the lacquer-laced fence girdering the chapel and the drywall of the reformed duplex, which memory serves originally contained a squash-court; tracing footsteps, in threes and fives, to the intersection of Frankston Ave. and Lowe Bvd., before stumbling across the threshold of our own homes, only to divorce ourselves of our neckties and go smoke cigarettes in the garage beneath the laundry.

It proved a starburst moment in the wizening story of our lives, the morning an impeccably-manicured agent in her marital attorney best stormed the steps of Luke Quinn O'Florin's brownstone artist's retreat, and peremptorily instructed Soleil to function as a mediator in greeting Quinn, whom the agent heralded as the 'new trend' of avant artistry – even the pioneer of such a movement. Quinn was as perplexed as we all were, and this perhaps prevailed as the point of contention we can admit aligned with Quinn's own, that he didn't consider himself the pioneer of anything; in fact, he couldn't fathom in entirety what unnavigable territory he was forging to explore if any, in painting his iconographic images of melancholy triangles and belligerent spheres, and that all the forty-piece installation which he'd been anguishing over the preceding year symbolised was an indulgent exercise in colour use; an exploratory creative goof, an ornate Cubist novelty which would only undermine the respect deigned him by those critics whom held him in high regard. This he murmured uncertainly, to the agent as she winningly slid down his balustrade and fell into the driver's seat of her electric blue Lamborghini, the axles of its tyres screaming in synchronicity to the clutch's doubletake as it was forced to propel itself from first to third gear. Quinn and Soleil watched her depart, and we watched them watch the residual smoke from the speeding engine as it lorded over the emptied side-street slate. When they caught our hunted, introspective eyes darting from between curtain-blinds and over the lip of brandished leafblowers, they too scrabbled inside, marking the parameters for our observation. Soleil might have shrieked aloud at our 'pornographic indecency', before being forgivably ushered behind closed door by Quinn, but we felt superior if we denied to ourselves that our complicit suburban espionage had ever been revealed. We exacted noble purpose in continuing on unabashedly, as though our lintels required dusting or our yards needed tending; but we never witnessed Quinn ball up the cheque the agent had offered him for his accumulated work.

We saw Soleil press it into a precise billfold, and then transfer this to Quinn's gesticulating hands. If we were Quinn, which we weren't and were lacking in the necessary social apparatus to demonstrate the same specie of genius, we would have taken the money, too. This wasn't a circumstance of pride, we reasoned. This was about embracing reward for what seemed rightly ours.

He first moved out of our neighbourhood on a turbid white day fat with haphazard summertime sleet, at the end of the next year, whilst the litterblown storm-drains of our streets were covertly sealed over by way of local council's decree, in an attempt to prevent neighbourhood cats from becoming ensnared during the heavy rains of September. We peered from between gardening shears and from beneath the corroded bodies of our automobiles, maintaining vigil as the laughing agreeable friends of Quinn and Soleil launched themselves down Quinn's adobe front-yard path eleven times that morning: shouldering an inventory of cardboard boxes taped fast, artfully evading the riot of thorned crocus sprouting from the vegetation sandbox clustering about the hinges of the squealing swing-gate immediately at the entrance to his property. We saw Soleil entwine arms round Quinn's back, and peer up with an unexpressed fury of gorgeous love, her chin jutting into the buttonholes of his tan suit jacket.

We saw him smile with a reverential vehemence, and mutter something more precious than swallows in a Rimbaud painting, right into the strawberry tresses of her hair. He slow-danced her, then, Quinn's fingers interlinking with her own, and we stared with such aching joy as his friends hooted, and encircled them with clattering applause amongst the boxes branded 'GARBAGE' and overflowing with waffle-toasters in disrepair and Britannica business planners now out-of-date, on the incline of Quinn's lawn. When they'd completed their sixth ballroom rotation, they collapsed into gleeful fits of eccentric laughter, and they all rattled into their friends' canary-yellow Coupe, like clowns into a stage-car.

Soleil didn't look over her shoulder, as we were compelled to hedge bets that she would. The car rounded the sharp left at the intersection of Lowe and Levinson, and we gazed without word as the suburban monarchy was transported away and melted into the drift of morning drizzle.

We went to our living rooms, clutched our abominable heads in our hands, and cried.

Soleil's ring-pool was later punctured and deflated by our children as they scattered over the asphalt to salvage the unwanted possessions of that naive Irish boy, sharp sticks aloft in their hands.

Missing

Ryan O'Neill

Look at that sky, you would think Christ was on his cross again, always no sun at all in this … this … damn it! This part of town. A torn sign on a wall of graffiti says C_M__ARY. It is similar to my mind, full of blanks. I walk round paths that wind through badly cut grass, looking and looking until I find a mound by a magnolia bush. I stand and pray, thinking of Adam, my husband. And I think of Sam, our son, our six-and-a-bit boy still crying for his dad. Sorrow is in my brain, I think, but not my soul, not in that thing, that what do you call it? I taught biology for so long, and now I can't think of a word for that pulpy thing with four small rooms, continually pumping blood around my body. I'm similar to diagrams I would draw in Biology class. A blank box would point to parts of a chalky body. My scholars (if I can in truth call such poor pupils that) had to fill in any vacant box with 'arm', 'shin', and so on. God, what is it? I can't think of any word for it.

Is that why I miss Adam in a niggling, trivial way, as if this was all child's play and my husband was only hiding, about to jump out with a boo? I am missing an important part, but I don't know what it is. I can miss Adam, but that's all. I know this idiotic lingo has a word for it, but it slips away. My poor brain. I start to cry now, not for my lost husband, but for words I can't say. Liquid runs down my skin and my lips, and I don't know what to call it, this sad damp. 'I miss you,' I say aloud.

At that instant a man stands at my arm, smart in a black suit, a suit you might put on to a burial. Or possibly put in for a burial. This man is old, sixty if a day, with a kind worn-out look about him, and a grin that turns into a frown as you look at it. 'I'm Paul. John's old man. Did you know my son?' that man says, staring at a curvy scar that runs up and down my cranium. (That right part of my skull has a disfiguringly long whitish scar stitching skin that carcrash glass cut away. I watch it in mirrors and shop windows, my scar changing as I study it. It is a c with a bar across it or an a rotating around, turning bottom loop to top.)

'No, I don't,' I say.

'Didn't. It's didn't now.'

'I'm sorry. What was his …?'

'John,' Paul cuts in angrily.

'Why do you ask?' I say.

'Why cry on this spot if you didn't know my son?'

'No, this isn't your son's …' I say, 'No, this is Adam's. My husband that was.'

'I'm sorry. It's a fault on your part,' Paul says, pointing to a flamboyant script giving Born and so on.

'I can't follow … I can't grasp it. I'm sorry. It says what?'

Obviously John's dad knows it without looking and says, 'John Smith, Born 1969 and …' poor Paul starts to sob.

'I'm sorry, I'll go,' I say and limp away. Adam was put in this ground, I know it, but I can't find him. Oh God, what kind of a woman am I? Raindrops drip down, blurring my sight. It suits this day's mood, as fitting as fictional rain in a plot by a hack author. That sky is crying for you, it says. How prosaic. I didn't throw dirt on Adam's coffin, but this world.

It's a rainy half hour of walking from c_m__ary to library. In this old (for Australia) building, that was a Masonic Hall long ago, I sit and look through a dictionary. On most days, that is, bar Saturday and Sunday, my days with Sam. Mondays I find most difficult, with Sam at school, so I visit Adam and following that, a library in this suburb or that. Ignoring Mr Williams, a librarian so stiff and wordy I think of a boring hardback book if thinking of him at all, I pass by him with only a 'good morning'. Mr Williams, writing in an indigo journal, says 'Morning' back. An hour of looking at kids' books, until I can work out that Spot runs, but not a lot apart than that. I ask Mr Williams for an Oxford Dictionary. (His photo is by 'librarian' in L, I laugh with him.) Finishing A and B and C and D this last month, now it is book 5 I want. But a gap proclaims that an unknown library patron has it out. Alright, F it is, though I am not fond of jumping forward. I want to find all my missing words. Thousands I was familiar with in days past. I try pulling words from this dictionary, cramming consonants and dipthongs into my mouth. I'm sick of not knowing what to call things. My world is full of what-do-you-call-its and thingummyjigs. I must approach around words. I subsist by synonyms and antonyms. I don't know what to call that sharp thing you cut with, so I say, 'I want a fork,' my noggin shaking, and my son brings a cutting thing. I am not a woman, not who I was, just a homonym of that individual. I favour books with 'I' narration, marking out my id with 'I's'. A long row of posts that surround a void. If I didn't know that I was missing parts ... Happy I. But as it is, I can't blank out all my blanks.

I sit by a giant dirty window and study F. Glancing out, I spot that it is not raining and a pallid sun is moving agonisingly slowly upwards, as if towards its own Golgotha. That's all for today. My scar is throbbing, my mouth dry and I swallow a handful of pills with a can of Coca Cola. A black for pain, a pink for forthcoming vomit, a brown for ... what did Burton call it?

Mr Williams frowns and points to a sign forbidding food and drink. I put back F. It's G I'm most looking forward to. I want to look up God, good, and so on. I borrow six books for my son and as I go out, Mr Williams looks sad, as if not borrowing him is disappointing. It isn't raining now and a trio of birds fly past a suspicion of sun coming through stormy clouds. Crows, I think. First for sorrow, two for joy and a third for a girl? No, it isn't a crow at all, but a bird that brings with it thoughts of maths. A mag? All my biology and I don't know what to call a common bird.

It's almost four now, and I must rush to school to pick up my son. I pass through a shopping mall, and a small man standing with a sign that says 'Christ was God's Word in Human Form.' This tiny man is shouting at anybody and nobody who walks by. It is not commonly I can know all words on a sign, and I stop to look at it, savouring this stirring in my mind. Calling to yours truly my holy man wants to start a discussion on faith and worship, two things I find ridiculous. Strolling away from him, I simply nod. 'You madam! God's word is in this book.' Brandishing his Christian holy book (what is it again? A Koran? I can't mind.) Angrily, I shout, 'What if a word or two is missing from your Good Book. How would you know? A mislaid instruction or fifty. Possibly a communication from Saint Paul to a handful of Corinthians, sanctifying a matching position in Christ's Church for a lady as for a man. Or proof that apocrypha is in fact, fact. How can you trust words? In actuality, isn't your book a work of fiction? As a biologist-'

'Oh, a biologist!' our saintly man mocks. 'Biology says nothing. You and I, our mums, dads, sons, cousins, starting from chimps? No! That's fiction! I trust in this book. I trust in Christ. I trust in words. John, chapt-'

'So long!' I say, and my holy man grins sadly and hands out a tract, 'God's Salvation,' which I put in my bag without looking at. I wish I could stay to study that sign, work out why I can know it so straightforwardly. Looking around I can't put a word to that shop in which I buy ham, pork, ribs, or, a narrow building that has on display in a window wanting washing, tabloids with photographs of Hollywood stars falling drunk out of cars.

At school, I wait for my son to finish his class. Boys and girls run round a bright playground in black uniforms. Sam is holding my hand now. I forgot a parting kiss on his hair this morning. Our shadows must touch, my son says. Walking back to our flat, hand in hand, Sam chats about school and pals and toys and words. Adam is in Sam, in Sam's worship of words. I mind Adam always filling in crosswords, composing lipograms, planning a grammar class for migrants from Afghanistan, Iran and Rwanda. Such riddling was too difficult for an ignorant biologist such as I. I still mind Adam's first words, so long ago. An autumn morning at uni, kookaburras kookaburring. I am sitting on a hard plastic chair, waiting for a bus. Adam is in front, playing with words in his journal. Glancing down, I study this striking young man, dividing, adding, subtracting and multiplying consonants. Noticing my look, this bold young man turns round and says, 'Madam, I'm Adam.' It was a thingummyjig, a pal-in-drum?

Adam is holy in Sam's mouth, a communion word. My son has a look of bliss saying it. I don't talk to him about his dad as much as I should. It's just that I can't say all that I want to say. On TV I saw that in a lost African clan, if a man or woman croaks (as Adam was fond of saying, for thoughts of mortality had my husband afraid, not wanting to dignify 'passing away') as I said, if an individual is shuffling off this mortal coil, a handful of words will vanish too. Adam took most of my words away into his coffin, worms gobbling words.

At our flat, I cook pasta for us. Sam is waiting to start our tutorial. I walk past a costly looking maroon book you can't avoid noticing on our dusty floorboards. It was this book that Adam was about to finish that night of our crash. 'La Dispirition.' Adam could study books in Français. I was always bad at any jargon but this.

'Mummy!' Sam says sharply and I sit by him. Pointing to an A in his book, my son says, 'What's this, Mummy?'

'A,' I say.

Now pointing to U.

'U.'

Sam indicating I.

'I.'

Now O.

'O.'

'And this?' Sam says.

'I … I don't know.'

It starts off as a sign for nothing and turns alarmingly into its own body. I'm afraid of it.

'It's OK, Mummy,' Sam says. 'Try writing now?'

I scrawl a handful of words. 'A quick brown fox jumps that lazy vicious dog.' 'Good, Mummy! But a small thing is missing, and it's not a consonant.' (How can such a young boy know such a word as consonant?) But I don't know what is missing. I start to cry.

'Wait, Mummy,' Sam says, and puts on my lap a card drawn at school. It is black, with big, clumsy pink writing. It says 'I ❤ you.' I hold this card to my body. ❤ is that word I was looking for this morning.

It is ❤ that stops us from dying. I know that now.

Movement & Noise

A. S. Patrić

The neighbourhood's children lived on the streets in summertime. A bowler would run up a driveway and fielders were ready to dive for catches on the nature strips or bitumen. Games of cricket could go on until there was barely enough light to see the ball. The boys had bikes and would ride in packs. In front of a given house you could see four or five bicycles, abandoned in a heap of tyres and metal tubing, silver spokes revolving when a breeze picked up – until the kids burst out of the front door and were off again.

There weren't many skateboards in that neighbourhood, but you'd be able to spot someone on roller skates. The owner of the local milk bar had bought his daughter a pair. White leather boots. Bright red rubber wheels. Sara was skinny and quiet but she loved to get some speed up on those roller skates. The boys rode past her like they were part of a gathering storm. They didn't stop to bother her and she barely noticed them. Sara's arms still grabbed at the air for balance but she was getting faster and smoother.

Her father came out of his milk bar late one summer afternoon. The boys were on the street, their bikes thrown across the hot bitumen. He walked over to tell them to pick up their damned bicycles and get off the road. They could be careless but he'd never seen them this disruptive.

Among the boys and their bikes was his daughter. They had gathered around her. Sara was lying on the ground as if she was asleep but the road was so hot the heat was radiating right up through his thongs.

Sebastian didn't get off his bike. He had his hands on the handlebars and a foot on one of the pedals. He had been out riding his BMX in the paddocks, around the new houses being built past Taylors Road, when Alex told him about Sara being run down.

The ambulance had been and gone. A police car was in front of the milk bar, the lights on top of the vehicle turning silently. Without a siren they seemed like carnival lights but they brought out a hush from the descending evening, a single breath being exhaled for hours.

The boys had their bikes on the road but cars driving through the neighbourhood didn't yell or beep for anyone to move out of the way. They did u-turns and chose other routes as if there was all the time in the world.

Sebastian parked his bike next to a fence and walked closer to the owner of the milk bar. Sebastian wondered what he was saying to the police but all he kept doing was repeating the same thing over and over – something that seemed pretty obvious to Sebastian.

No-one had witnessed Sara get run over but the police had noted the damage to her legs and head, and had told her father that the vehicle was moving well above the speed limit. Sara's father kept asking them why would the driver race away without telling anyone? Why would someone keep driving? Why just drive away? How could he do that?

His daughter might have been laying there on the hot road for minutes before she died.

Sebastian wanted to tell the milk bar owner that the man in the car would have been scared and that he wanted to get away without anyone knowing. Running away was something Sebastian did sometimes but he didn't understand the man's question. It couldn't be that simple. Not if it was repeated so many times.

As the owner of the milk bar, Sara's dad could often be found standing at his counter, leaning over an open newspaper. He offered commentary with a finger pressed down on an article. He saw terrible things happening every day and sold the proof to his customers, so it was baffling that he couldn't understand something as basic as a hit and run. Maybe what he meant was that they could have called an ambulance earlier if the man had stopped. They could have taken his daughter to the hospital together. That hadn't happened and Sara's dad kept repeating his question as if he would never ever stop.

When Sebastian went home he didn't tell his father about the accident. Ivan got angry if he was asked questions or if he was told useless information or if he was distracted. At the moment he was sitting at the kitchen table with the radio tuned to a news show. He didn't ever seem to pay attention to it.

Sebastian thought about those silent police lights turning in the fading light of the long hot day and it occurred to him that his father didn't like silence. It barely mattered what the news on the radio was. Ivan just wanted to hear voices as though the house was full of friends.

Ivan had his shoe box out and a chess set beside it. Within the box were hundreds of clippings from the newspapers. Each strip of newspaper had a chess problem. Ivan dwelled on these puzzles for hours in the evenings. Eventually, he would reach out a careful hand and move one of the pieces on his specially configured board.

Sebastian opened a can of chocolate Quick. It had the foil at the top so he ran a spoon around the inside of the circle and made sure he pulled out every bit of the foil.

Ivan talked over his shoulder at him, 'Only three.'

Meaning that many teaspoons because Ivan had seen five or six spooned into a mug in the past. Sebastian knew the rule, but he heaped the three spoons as high as he could and Ivan didn't notice. Ivan only listened for the three clinks of metal against ceramic, and let his son slurp while he drank the chocolate milk.

Sebastian's dad reassembled the pieces on the chess board to the original configuration of the problem printed on the slip of newspaper and started again. Often he did this all night with just the one clipping.

Sebastian turned off the radio. Ivan looked up and was angry until Sebastian said he was ready to play chess. Ivan smiled instead of yelling and waved his hand at the board like a magician.

Sebastian chose one of his father's raised fists and it revealed a black pawn. They began resetting the board – Ivan quick, stamping down the white pieces – Sebastian slowly, placing all of his black pieces in the exact middle of their squares. He loved resetting the board and his dad let him take his time. Sebastian adjusted all his father's pieces because some of them were almost in other files or ranks.

They played every day but Sebastian's progress was measured by how many moves he survived rather than victories. His greatest moment had been playing his father through to a stalemate. Sebastian still couldn't understand how he'd managed to draw. Ivan was probably distracted. Yesterday's game had lasted an admirable amount of moves (thirty-five or thirty-six) before Ivan checkmated his son with an intricate combination of pawns and a bishop. Sebastian was hoping to better that today.

The house was quiet, the birds outside could be heard in the trees. Sebastian could hear Jet barking from Alex's backyard, and that was on the other side of the block. If Sebastian's brother was home his music would have been playing. Derek locked himself in his room and played Springsteen or Led Zeppelin, The Doors or Hendrix, so loud sometimes the windows trembled. Sebastian didn't like his father's radio solution to the silence or his brother's noise, but he didn't want the house to be so quiet either. It was like that police light outside the milk bar today, turning noiselessly, except they couldn't even see the red and blue lights in their house. They just felt the siren when all the noise was turned off.

Ivan beat his son in twelve moves and then told him to go outside and get lemons from their lemon tree because they were having fish tonight. Sebastian was disappointed not to have survived the opening sequence. He wanted to reset the pieces and start again. He daydreamed of going one better than a stalemate. Not so much the winning part of it, but he liked the idea of beating his father at chess, and then refusing to play him ever again afterwards. That's what Derek had done. Now he never played chess, not even when Sebastian begged him for a game.

'Now!' said his dad.

There was a bundle of white paper in the fridge that Derek must have brought from the butchery. He'd been working there for years and had finished being an apprentice – though he never called himself a butcher. It was just a way to make money, and Derek saved every cent of it for the day he was going to get his license. That was just a few days away now and he'd already bought an old Mustang. He was still saving so he could paint it midnight blue.

Sebastian drained the last of his chocolate milk. He used the teaspoon to get to the undissolved powder at the bottom. He washed out the mug. If he didn't, his dad would shout at him. Ivan might stand up and slap the back of Sebastian's head. That looked funny in the movies but in real life it hurt a lot.

Sebastian shook off his wet fingers as he walked away from the sink. Before he could leave the kitchen, Ivan told him to go to the garage and tell his brother to finish whatever he was doing with the damned car and come inside. They needed to put dinner on and Derek had been cooking since Mum went away. She was trying to get better so she could be their mother again but that might take another few months.

Derek would be in the garage. When he wasn't playing loud music in his bedroom he was in the garage with his tools and his car. Sebastian got a bottle of Coke out of the fridge to take to his brother.

Sebastian went outside and felt the dry, baking heat of the day roll back over him. Strange how it could still be so hot, even without the sun in the sky. The heat was now in the concrete and bricks, the air and the ground. He yelled out for Derek but he didn't hear him call back.

Sebastian expected to find him polishing his car or under the hood doing something to the engine, but he wasn't working on the Mustang tonight.

Tonight, Derek was sitting inside the car with his hands on the wheel. He used to daydream and pretend he was driving, even just a few weeks ago in Dad's car, but then he'd step out and get on his push bike like the rest of the kids in the neighbourhood.

The heat in the garage was intense and the driver's side window was open. Derek sat there with his hands on the wheel, sweat pouring down his face as if he'd been running for hours. It was falling from his nose and chin, and he was not playing his music. His Mustang made a dripping noise as water from the radiator splashed onto the concrete.

Flat Daddy

Louise D'Arcy

Flat Daddy goes everywhere with you. Flat Daddy sits on the chair next to you and stares outwards, but still looking at you out of the corner of his eye. Flat Daddy sometimes gets left behind in the wrong room and has to be fetched. That feels bad and no-one laughs, though everyone wants to.

You can't go around the back of Flat Daddy. That way you see the bits of tape and the yellowy foam like someone peed on it. Flat Daddy's best from the front. If you sit him on the floor and lean him against a chair you can hug him and kiss him right on the lips. That felt kind of strange at first, and I had to work out how to do it.

When your friends come round, they want to do it too but you can't let them. That means you can't leave them in the room with him or they'll do it when you're not there.

So they have to come to the toilet with you and to the kitchen and to the front door when it rings. Sometimes Flat Daddy comes too, though not to the toilet. He came to watch in the bath once but he got wet and that got me into big trouble. He was taken downstairs and I wasn't allowed to take him out of the front room for the rest of the week.

Flat Daddy nearly went in to school on Family Day but in the end he stayed in the car. Everyone went out to the car park to look at him and then we had to open a window a little way or he'd die from lack of oxygen. That made people very excited and someone cried. Flat Daddy just looked right out through the windshield like they weren't there.

Cindy loves her Flat Daddy. Matter of fact it was a real issue at first. I found myself fighting with a nine-year old, sneaking around trying to get a hold of him when she wasn't looking. Except she always was. Can't get her to concentrate on any job for twenty seconds but move Flat Daddy an inch and she knows it.

Then I worked out it was easier knowing where Flat Daddy was. Well, knowing where he wasn't, to tell you the exact truth. If he was in the lounge with Cindy and her friends then he wasn't out on the back porch with me and the girls drinking beer. That way I didn't need to worry him about it. Erica wanted to bring him out to share a beer with us but Erica can go too far if you don't watch that girl. Flat Daddy would end up with a beer moustache and stains all down his front if you left things to her. I reckon it's much better he stays inside with Cindy playing school and tea parties.

He has to sit at the head of the table when we eat. Don't know why – we always eat in front of the tv when it's just the two of us. Cindy likes to serve him up the same as us. I have to cook what he likes and we can't start eating till he's said Grace.

The first time I told her Flat Daddy can't say Grace she gave me a look. She gets that from her daddy, that look, the one that nearly fries your butt off. Don't look at me like that, I said and she looked right back and said, Don't tell me what to do, you stinking whore, and then we both cried and pretended it never happened. That night Cindy hugged me in bed so tight I could hardly breathe. I had to stay till she fell asleep and my leg went numb and it gave way when I was trying to slip off the bed quietly.

Flat Daddy gets to go outside now it's warmer and the grass is dry. He leans against the swing and I can touch him on the top of his head every time I swing past. Real Daddy has blonde hair that sticks up but you can't tell that from looking at Flat Daddy. Flat Daddy looks like he's got a smooth top. When Real Daddy comes home I'll tell him to cut his hair like that and put some gel on it.

I talk to Flat Daddy a lot, especially last thing at night when the lights are off and all I can hear are the cars going by outside. Flat Daddy listens like he's really listening. Even though I can't see him I know he's looking straight ahead but not seeing anything, just paying close attention to what I'm saying.

And I can say anything at all, he doesn't mind. I told him what happened last Christmas after he went out and came back in next day with the flowers and the chocolates. Maybe he doesn't remember. Sometimes Real Daddy didn't remember stuff and told me I was making up stories again, like making up stories is a bad thing.

My friends got bored with Flat Daddy real quick. They won't let me bring him outside any more, they say I'm showing off, like I'm something special. Unless I'm playing by myself I leave him on the chair beside my bed.

Cindy left Flat Daddy out last night. It rained and he looks kind of wrinkly now. Poor kid. When she looked out of the window and saw him there, leaning against the swing, she screamed and ran and hid in the laundry. When I looked out to see what it was I saw he had one of her grandma's woolly hats on his head. That did it for me - I laughed and laughed. Cindy came out eventually to see what the noise was all about. She hugged me again, tight round the waist, which is as high as she can reach. I picked her up and squeezed her back. I'm not mad, I said, when I could get the words out. You reckon? she says right back.

We got the letter today. I didn't open it till Cindy left for school, thank God. I gave it to Flat Daddy to read, see if he could make more sense of it than I could. He just stared out the window and I did too.

Erica came round at lunchtime and found us still there. She read the letter and cried. I've never seen Erica cry before. I'm so sorry, so sorry, she kept saying, which wasn't much help to me so I got up and left her and Flat Daddy together.

Will Flat Daddy come to the funeral? asks Cindy that night, real late, after we'd sat up together on the couch with Flat Daddy between us. Don't see why not, I say, knowing it'll cause an almighty row with his folks. Mind you, I can get one of them just breathing. Great idea, Cind', I say. She takes Flat Daddy up to bed and when I go up later I hear her singing lullabies to him. He's lying in her bed under the covers and she's sitting beside him stroking his head.

Can't get rid of Erica these days. She wants to know what we're planning for the funeral. I don't know yet, I tell her, we don't even know when we're getting the body, what's the rush? He likes things to be right, she says, like I don't know that. Seems to me, I said, you care a lot more about this funeral than I do. She didn't come round for a few days after that.

When I see her next, down at the supermarket, she looks terrible. No makeup, no tight jeans. And without them, no wiggle when she walks. I'm sorry, she says again when she sees me. But this time it's a different sorry, one that means something to me. No sweat, Erica, I tell her, I know you loved him, too. She looks at me then, properly, and I see crow's feet round her eyes I've never noticed before. She must have always had them buried under foundation. Still, I kind of like her better without. You feel like you're talking to the real person. Then she goes and hugs me. She's never done that before. Thought she wasn't going to let go. In the end I have to kind of shrug her off and she just runs out the door. Must be her time of the month.

People want to know how he died. They keep asking and

I have to keep saying I don't know. Gets kind of annoying, to tell you the truth. Classified information, I say, they won't even tell me, and they look at me like I haven't tried hard enough to find out.

'But he's back!'

That was Mrs Forrest down at the corner store. She looked out of the door and saw him there in the front seat of the car staring right back at her. I turned round real fast at that, twirled round on my heel and looked, like she might be right. Someone screamed but I just saw the funny side of it. Mrs Forrest took that real bad. Guess I'll have to get my milk and bread someplace else now.

Cindy wants to put some of her daddy's real clothes on Flat Daddy now it's getting cold. Had to tell her grandma came and took all his clothes away, the day we took Flat Daddy to the mountains. All she left was a sock lying at the back of the wardrobe. What? she says, Why? Who? I say right back, Where? That makes her laugh.

It seems people don't want you to laugh. Even Erica doesn't seem to like it much. She came round the other night and wouldn't have a beer, wouldn't have anything. Wouldn't really speak. What's up? I said, taking a slug of my own. Don't you think drinking on your own's kinda cheap? she says. Now Erica's many things, but a class act she isn't. What the hell would you know? I say. You never loved him, she says, like she was in the middle of a different conversation altogether, and she grabbed him up and hugged him, right there in front of me. Cindy's right, Flat Daddy from the back is not a good look.

Put him down you stinking whore! That was Cind' again. Erica put him down then and looked like she was about to take a swing at Cindy. Get out, I said, real calm, we don't want you here, and me and Cind' went and watched some TV. Eventually we heard her go, we heard the screen door slam and the car fire up. When I went in later to clear up before I went to bed, I found Flat Daddy was gone.

Strange thing is, I miss that Flat Daddy, pee-stained foam and everything. More than Cindy does. Let's get a cat, I said to Cindy, cats are good at staring. Yeah, OK, she says, like it's no big deal, which it is, her daddy never allowed her a pet. I'll be too busy to look after it, though, she says, like she's some hotshot business executive.

Flat Daddy's gone. My friends don't ask about him any more, so I don't even tell them. They think he's still here, sitting on my bedside chair listening to me. And that's just dumb. When the kitten comes they'll want to come round to see it, I bet. If I let them. I'll tell them about Flat Daddy then. Tell them he went to live with Erica, just like the real daddy said he was going to do when he got home.

How My Father Dies in the End

Patrick Cullen

My father didn't die the night he left my mother and me alone in our house on the outskirts of town. No, he did not die then. Instead, he left my mother for a woman he'd met in the office where he worked. It was his job to watch over the hours kept by construction workers; it was not his job to reluctantly dole out their wages as though they came from his own pocket, but it's said that that's how he did it. Like my father, the woman – the daughter of the man who owned the construction business – was married at the time. But maybe she was more inclined to leave her own marriage because it was without children and the pleasure they are supposed to bring.

What happened – all that really happened – was that after he left I lay in the darkness of my room, wondering if it was not something between my father and the other woman, or between my father and my mother but, instead, something between my father and me.

He may have left that night but he did not die, not then.

He died a week later, the day of my tenth birthday. At the urging of my mother – 'Whatever you want!' – I had made my birthday wish and I imagined that she'd be as pleased as I was if my wish – the return of my father – was granted.

But that morning, I crept down the hall and found my mother alone and weeping in her bed. I knew that the day I faced at school was one of awkwardness, and that the awkwardness would follow me after school and into a party with friends who would already know – just a week later – that I was from a 'broken' home and – even at the ages of nine and ten themselves – know that it meant something. Something big and insufferable.

Rather than suffer the likely day ahead, I feigned illness: stomach cramps, intense but widespread; something hard to pin down, and less pointed than the hint of appendicitis. My mother had to work that day, and I knew that there was no one on whom she could call to care for me. The greatest suffering, for both of us, was those few seconds she hovered beside my bed, that awful expression on her face as she weighed up what she would lose – or if she would even gain something – by not going to work. And my greatest joy was when she drove away; I'd never felt better. She left me with more space and silence and solitude than I had ever known. I wandered around the house, entering rooms as though for the first time. The newness of things was fixed in those moments and in those same moments disappearing, because as I left each room I felt that I would never return.

In the bathroom, the prints of my father's fingers were smeared across the mirror from when he'd last lost himself there amid the steam. In the lounge room, the indentations of his shoes were still in the carpet, emerging from the kitchen linoleum and disappearing out onto the concrete verandah. I walked backwards through the room, reversing over his prints with long clumsy strides, until I was in the kitchen. There I saw the scuff of his shoes on the linoleum and followed it through the room to the laundry and, from the laundry, around to where his dull markings morphed into prints blurred in the hallway carpet. I continued backwards in his footsteps until I reached my parents' – my mother's – bedroom.

The impression of my mother's head was still on her pillow, and on the far side of the bed, the side on which he had slept, there was no trace of my father. I had always known that to be his side of the bed and I remembered, then, what had always been under that side. I crossed the room and kneeled beside the bed and grinned foolishly, so surprised I was – no, relieved – to find that it was still there.

On my tenth birthday, I slid my father's rifle out from under my parents' bed, opened the drawer of the bedside table and took out a thin cardboard box, the bullets tinkling like loose change as I tipped them out onto the covers. Still dressed in my pyjamas, I stood in my parents' bedroom and briefly thought about what had happened in my own small life, and in that moment it made perfect sense that leaving was sometimes the best thing to do. So, I loaded the rifle and went out into the backyard.

I stood there struggling under the rifle's weight, my cheek against the stock like my father had taught me, and I sighted every window in that empty house. I sighted each window and I watched. I waited for him to show his goddamn face – I wanted him to; if he was ever to return then that was surely his moment, but he was not there for me.

My shoulder burned. The rifle became too much and the tip of the barrel fell forward, digging into the ground. I inverted the rifle and placed the butt of the stock between my bare feet and picked long blades of grass from the barrel. It reminded me of toy rifles I'd seen on television, on shows.

I'd watched with my father, back when he got home from work on time – the trigger was pulled and, after a puff of harmless smoke, a little flag would unfurl: Bang! Ha, ha. You're dead. Joke's on you. And everyone would laugh – my dad and me together.

Alone in the backyard, with the tip of the barrel right there in front of my face, I slid my hand down onto the trigger and I stared into that dark hole and fired. Ha, ha, Dad. Joke's on you.

My father died much later, after days, weeks, months of suffering. By then his new girlfriend had left him – and not for anyone else either: she'd just left him.

He drank and smoked more than ever, and he did nothing to look after himself. He got cancer and ended up in hospital. He called my mother, desperate to have someone with him, and I heard her tell him that he'd made his own bed and it was time that he lay in it – even if he was going to have to lie in it alone.

But my mother did go and see him over his final weeks. 'Only because he's dying,' she told me. His cancer was what the doctors called fungating. My mother said to think of it as a cancer that comes out of you, and at night I would lie in my bed with my hand inside my pyjama top, knuckles pushing out between the buttons, my fist like an alien bursting out of my stomach. The thought of him dying like that used to make me laugh. Ha, ha. You're dead.

No. My father didn't die then. My father died years later, during the Gulf War. He'd gone there as a reporter, and a convoy in which he travelled came under fire and my father was the only one to survive. He was captured, held for months and for much of that time we knew nothing – my mother was only told that he was missing. And then, one night as I sat mulling over some geography homework, there he was: barely recognisable because of the beard he'd grown or, rather, had been unable to shave off. He was saying that the war was wrong and that he would rather die for his mistake than come home to his own family. And then a man stepped into the frame and the footage froze as a pistol was held to my father's head. I waited for a flag to unfurl from the barrel; I really thought it would, but it didn't. No matter how many times that scene was replayed, there was no flag, no Bang!, no Ha, ha. My father died a victim of his circumstances.

He died a joke that had lost its punchline.

No, my father didn't die like that. He died much more simply. He died on my first day at high school as I walked through the maze of corridors and lockers and hormones. He died when my first girlfriend's friend told me that … like … she – my girlfriend – didn't want to be my girlfriend anymore and that she – my girlfriend (but maybe her friend too) – wasn't sure if she ever really did … like … want to be my girlfriend. He died when I first turned the key in the ignition of the car in which he himself had learned to drive. He died the first time I ever drove that car alone, and every time I drove some girl – usually an ex-girlfriend's friend – someplace to be alone with her, knowing that she would make me feel that if I died that night I'd at least die happy.

My father died more times than I can remember: he died the night he left my mother and me alone in our house. He died each and every time I was injured or afraid or for some reason felt that life was not worth living. He died each time I was ever a failure at anything, and he still died any time I was ever a success at something. And he died one last time the night my own son was born. That night, as I cradled my son against my chest, in awe of how he could be so small and fragile and so in need, I knew in the space of one tiny breath that I could lay down my own life for him: I knew then that a father could die for his son and, if he could, he would do it more than once.

My father still lives in the town where we were both born, the town where he has spent his whole life and where I spent all the years of my childhood – all of what I jokingly call my … like … deformative years. Ha, ha. I haven't been home for so long, and I can't imagine a time when I'll ever return.

In the end my father will surely die, and when he does he will die not knowing how I wished he'd lived.

The Sea Monkeys

Erol Engin

The Sea Monkeys were a birthday gift.

A shit birthday gift, it seemed.

'What are they, Daddy?' James asked, frowning.

It was Good Friday. Osmond watched his son stare at the plastic container and the food packet and the Magic Sea Monkey powder that he held in his hand. He held these things, Osmond noticed, a fair way from his body, and not right in front of his nose, which he would have done, had his interest been genuinely piqued by the gift. Osmond tried not to think it, but his little boy's body language said to him, loud and clear, 'Daddy's gift is weird and shitty.'

To make matters worse, Osmond declared, 'They're Sea Monkeys' in a voice beyond all reasonable enthusiasm, even for a birthday morning.

'But monkeys don't live in the sea,' replied James. 'And where are their mummies and daddies?'

'Well, James,' Osmond started, in a more subdued register, but was cut off by his son.

'Call me Jim, Daddy.'

'Well, Jim, they're not really monkeys. They're … they're …'

Osmond scrambled for the box. What the fuck were they?

But he had lost the moment. James had turned to the next gift, and the Sea Monkey kit was discarded into the burial ground of wrapping paper that surrounded him.

Osmond looked to Molly, his wife, for help, but she was too engrossed in her iPad.

'Can I open Mummy's gifts now, Daddy?'

Osmond nodded. Thoroughly routed, he retreated to the kitchen to pour another coffee.

Molly followed him in.

'At least you didn't get me a shit gift,' she said, brandishing her iPad. He'd given it to her two weeks ago, on her own birthday, her fortieth, against his better instincts. 'Then you'd really be in trouble.'

When no one was looking, Osmond rescued the Sea Monkey kit and followed the instructions with the utmost fidelity. He placed them in the living room on top of a buffet, just out of direct sunlight but not in the dark. And over the next few days, he checked the container with a dutiful regularity that bordered on the religious. His zeal, however, did not rub off on his family. It seemed that the proto-life forms incubating or gestating or whatever it was they were doing in the container held no magic for them. But Osmond was determined to ignite a spark of wonder in his son's eyes if it killed him.

On the third day, Easter Monday, the Sea Monkeys rose. It was almost biblical, really. Osmond couldn't wait to see the little saviours, the newly risen products of an, if not immaculate, conception, then at least a mysterious one. He ran downstairs to the buffet, and was rewarded with a show that he'd wished to see all his life. His mouth actually formed into an 'O' of wonder as he watched little pinkish specks flit about inside the container. They turned merry somersaults, performed agile back flips; they darted, plunged, winnowed, and entertained. They did everything that the ads in the comic books from his childhood said they would do. They were not a rip \[off, like his parents had always said they would be. And there had to be at least thirty little wriggly delights in there, Osmond guessed, perhaps more. Talk about value for money!

'James!' he called. 'James, get down here! Quick!'

A minute later a sleepy-eyed James, decked out in his glow-in-the-dark T-Rex pyjamas (one of Molly's gifts, a big hit), came padding downstairs.

'Call me Jim, Daddy. What is it?' he asked, his voice rising with interest.

Shuffling over, James blinked and rubbed the sleep from his eyes. He peered into the container. Osmond watched him intently.

'Pretty small,' he said, eventually.

'They'll grow,' said Osmond, too quickly. He couldn't say that James was exactly keen, but 'pretty small' was a fairly encouraging judgement.

'Do you want to feed them?'

'I have to feed them?' asked James, resentfully, as if being suckered into a raw deal.

'If you want them to live.'

James wobbled his head noncommittally, but Osmond thrust the packet at him.

'Use the small scoop,' he instructed. 'And you mustn't overfeed them. If you do, they'll die.'

James reflected for a moment and then said, 'Why can't I just have some fish, daddy?'

'Well …'

Osmond didn't know. He didn't know why James couldn't have fish. Why the fuck would anyone, for that matter, want Sea Monkeys when you could actually have fish? This brought a point home to Osmond. What he really wanted to explain, what was really at stake, was that for him, Sea Monkeys were associated in his memory with the youthful and carefree 1970s, for which he was growing increasingly, and quite pathetically, wistful.

He'd come across them in an Australian Geographic store, and the mere sight of the package showing the little crowned aquatic marvels transported him back to his childhood in Newcastle. He'd never actually owned any, or knew anyone who had, but that wasn't the point. He had stood almost transfixed by his discovery, and realised that this was better than his childhood. Now, he was the adult, the one with the money, the one with the ability to choose. No one could tell him they were a rip off. He could see for himself. As he picked the package off the shelf, Osmond knew that what he was doing was exceedingly rare, that this was a momentous occasion to which, it seemed, his whole life had been heading; a singular occasion in which past and present, child and adult, fused into one glorious, synergistic moment. And his son, his son would be the beneficiary of this … serendipity.

How could he possibly explain all this?

He couldn't.

The Sea Monkeys would have to do it for him.

'What's going on?' asked Molly, still in bed.

'Nothing,' yawned James.

'What?' said Osmond. 'You call these Little Wonders nothing?'

'What is it?' came the voice again from upstairs.

'Just the Sea Monkeys,' said James. 'Daddy's excited because they hatched.'

Molly clumped downstairs, yawning, iPad in hand. She shuffled over to the Sea Monkeys, peering down at them.

'Pretty small,' she said.

'That's what I said, Mummy.'

'They look like those icky little squiggly things that form in puddles. Yeccch.'

'They do not,' said Osmond, getting defensive. 'And as I already said, they'll get bigger.'

'How big?' asked James.

'The box says three-quarters of an inch.'

Using his fingers, Osmond showed his son how big three quarters of an inch was.

'They can't all grow that big,' said James. 'Not in that little container.'

'They probably won't all live,' Osmond explained, venturing into dangerous waters.

'Where will the dead ones go when they die?'

Osmond knew he was flirting with disaster. Under no circumstances, he told himself, should he respond with 'to Sea Monkey heaven'. This platitude, he knew, would be seized upon, thrashed, and torn apart by his son, who seemed to lie in wait for such slip-ups. So he shrugged his shoulders and said, atheistically, 'Don't know. No one knows where living things go when they die. They just die. And that's that.'

James nodded, satisfied with Osmond's realism. Osmond was about to add to his success when his son surprised him with another question.

'Can I take the Sea Monkeys to school tomorrow, Daddy? For News Day?'

Osmond smiled. Now this, he thought, was more like it.

Together, they spent much of the day collecting facts from the net about Sea Monkeys, which James could impart to his class. Father and son did hit the odd snag, particularly when they discovered that Sea Monkeys appeared to have mastered the secret of life after death. If numbers dwindled, all you had to do was aerate the water for a few days and they would somehow reappear.

'Like Jesus,' said Osmond, with delicious irreverence, before he could stop himself.

He didn't think James had heard, but he was wrong. It took a lengthy disquisition about how the Sea Monkeys were definitely not like Jesus before James let him off the hook.

Later in the evening, relaxing in bed with Molly, and feeling frisky, Osmond looked back on what he had done, and thought that it was good.

'He's a great kid,' he said, savouring a chocolate Easter egg. 'Really bright. I doubt if I would have asked where Sea Monkeys went when they died. In fact, I doubt if any kid I knew in the 70s would have asked that question. What a bunch of clods we were.'

Lately, whatever he said to Molly, no matter how interesting or close to his heart, sounded specious the moment he'd uttered it. He blamed Steve Jobs, the ghost of whom Molly took to bed each night, in the form of his creation, the iPad. And like Obi Wan Kenobi, Jobs seemed more powerful in death than he'd ever been in life. Next to such a wonder device Osmond felt dull and inadequate. How could he possibly have something of interest to say that couldn't be topped or outright demolished by her erudite new toy?

But tonight, it seemed that he'd bested his rival. Molly put the iPad down beside her, and turned to face him.

'Why did you say that about Jesus? It's not like you.'

Osmond shrugged. 'Blame it on all this Easter business.'

Molly laughed. 'It was great to watch you two this weekend. You really connected with him.'

She took a bite of his egg.

'And now,' she said, 'I want to connect with you.'

They made love for the first time in more than a month. It was only in the morning, when he nearly stepped on it, that Osmond noticed a vanquished iPad on the floor next to the bed.

'How do you like me now, Steve?' he bragged, before heading to the toilet.

At breakfast the next day Osmond fine-tuned James' News Day speech before taking him over to the school. James clutched the Sea Monkeys to his chest as they walked into the playground. It gratified Osmond to see that the Sea Monkeys were a big hit. Kids jostled one another to see what James was carrying; soon it seemed that half the school was bobbing and weaving around them. It was a while before the venerable Sea Monkeys and their acolytes made it safely to the classroom. With a final hug and kiss, a triumphant Osmond took leave of his son.

He sat in traffic, reflecting on the past six years. It had not been an easy road. Children are a wedge, a friend had once said, a wedge that will pry you and Molly apart. Be wary of this. Like all fathers-to-be, Osmond had summarily rejected this party-pooping advice. But with the passage of time he had been forced to revise his opinion. And just lately, the words seemed eerily Delphic in their prescience. A Wedge had indeed been driven between them. And the Wedge was multi-faceted. It doubled as a clear (and ubiquitous) demarcation between before and after, between a carefree youth and parental responsibility, between sex and no sex, and, when he felt particularly low, between All Things Good and All Things Bad. And the great problem was that he and Molly loved said Wedge, even more than they loved one another.

Osmond nodded at the sagacity of his thinking. But he didn't want this day spoiled. He sailed on to work, where he enjoyed a very un-Tuesday-like Tuesday. To Osmond, the day seemed sparkly and fresh, as did his co-workers, his contracts, and, indeed, himself. Could the Sea Monkeys have given him a new lease on life?

It was after lunch when Osmond answered his mobile.

And in a few short minutes, the day, and life in general, lost its glamour.

When Osmond got to the school, he found Molly and James, the principal and another teacher, a large woman with a beehive hairdo, sitting in an office, waiting for him. 'What took you?' asked Molly, clearly pissed off, either with him or the meeting or more likely both.

'Traffic,' he said, shrugging his shoulders. 'Now, what's up?'

The woman in the beehive hairdo, who happened to be American, answered him in what sounded like an Alabama drawl.

'Your son has been making inappropriate comments in mah Scriptures clay-yassss.'

Osmond had forgotten that Tuesday was also Scriptures day. He had also forgotten that James and this Confederate fossil from the 50s had crossed spiritual swords before.

'Is that true, James?' Osmond asked.

'God doesn't exist.'

'What?'

'God doesn't exist.'

'You all see?' said the woman with the beehive.

'What do you mean? What are you talking about, James?'

'Jim, Daddy. Sea Monkeys prove that God doesn't exist. They come from a packet, don't they?'

Osmond nodded.

'They don't come from God. God didn't make them. Alma says that everything comes from God.'

'Well now …'

'Maybe we come from a packet, too, and the packet says Humans instead of Sea Monkeys.'

'Don't be silly now,' said Osmond, 'let's …'

'Osmond,' said Molly, 'Jim's not being silly. He's just exploring the issue. You and this 'teacher' are squashing his interest and self-expression.'

Osmond closed his eyes and took a deep breath.

'Sir,' said the teacher, 'in mah opinion, those things you bought your son are of the Devil. Let me tell you what your son said. Your son said that those little things are like Our Lord and Saviour Jesus Christ.'

Osmond looked perplexed.

The principal, trying to act as the voice of reason, explained, 'It seems that your son made a speech in Scriptures about how these ... Sea Monkeys ... and Jesus are somehow alike. Do you know how he might have written such a speech?'

Osmond shook his head.

James was appalled. 'You said, Daddy, you said, remember? The Sea Monkeys are like Jesus! They can come back from the dead, too.'

Osmond was forced to come clean.

'I said something to that effect, yes, but as a joke. An ill-advised joke, to be sure, but still a joke.'

Osmond felt the accusing gaze of the principal and teacher, a gaze which said, quite clearly, What kind of idiot says that in front of his kid? They forced him to admit that he and James had indeed drafted a speech together. But, in his defence, Osmond pleaded that the speech had been meant for News Day, not for Scriptures. James, it seemed, bright boy that he was, must have adapted the speech for his own purposes, and thrown in a stupid off-hand comment from his father for good measure.

'Kind of impressive, really,' Osmond said.

The principal and the teacher did not share Osmond's viewpoint.

The meeting wore on, painfully. Molly argued heatedly in favour of Ethics over Scriptures, until it was finally decided that James, or Jim, rather, might spend Scriptures time more profitably by colouring-in for an hour? This seemed to suit all parties, and the meeting broke up with expressions of forced harmony and well-being.

That evening, after James went to bed, Molly, still fuming, instructed Osmond to get rid of those fucking monkey things. They would just remind her, she said, of the whole sorry weekend. But Osmond advised against haste.

'You wanted an excuse to get James out of Scriptures,' he said, when they were both in bed. 'Well, the Sea Monkeys were it.'

But it was not Osmond's night.

It was Steve Jobs'.

James didn't go to Scriptures, but if that solved one problem, it created another. Teased by other kids for being different, James toughed it out at school, but when Osmond picked him up each day, he broke down and wailed in the car all the way home. The Sea Monkeys, it seemed, had scarred him for life.

Osmond admitted that they had to go, but he hadn't the heart to get rid of them. They sat on the buffet, neglected, for a week, and when Osmond checked them on Sunday evening, there was only one lonely little squiggle left. It made circles in the water that seemed perfunctory at best. He watched it for a while. Sometimes it slowed down and peered out at him with its three crowns that looked like little black eyeballs, eyeballs that seemed to implore him to put it out of its misery, and to say, 'we tried our best, mate, but isn't it time we ended this impossible little dream of ours?'

The next day, Osmond checked on the lone Sea Monkey before going to work, to see how it was making out.

The squiggle was gone.

'Daddy,' James said, looking at the depleted container, 'could I have some fish?'

Osmond nodded.

'Yay!' James skipped off to tell Molly that Daddy had finally come to his senses.

What had he been thinking? What had he expected his clever son to do, sit staring at the things, like some simple-minded moron, as they went round and round their slimy fucking container? He had to admit that Sea Monkeys belonged to a bygone age, the age of tube socks and Star Wars and innocence, not the age of iPads and PlayStations and atheistic children.

Osmond seized the container and walked through the house. He was about to pour the Sea Monkey water into the toilet when, quite suddenly, he was struck by a vision. He saw himself smuggling the Sea Monkey container to work. He saw himself carefully aerating it. He saw a crowd of worshippers at his desk, staring in awe and wonder at the miracle transpiring before their eyes. For inside the grail of holy Sea Monkey water a newly regenerated batch of wonder creatures danced and cavorted.

The vision vested Osmond with the power to prove, once and for all, that Sea Monkeys were not a shit gift. They were a gift that could resurrect itself.

Like Jesus.

Get Smart

Bel Woods

You're in denial. You have to accept this. Even without the label – he's not going to be like everyone else.

I've trained my eyes to recognise him, even in a crowd of many children, wearing the same grey uniforms, with the same hazy hair colour, cut so similar. I concentrate, waiting for him to break from the blundering sea with his own erratic running style. I need to do this in case I forget his face – sometimes, I think, this could happen. He glows at me with cheeks flushed, missing teeth, something yellow on the front of his shirt. I hear the voices of the other mothers: 'I would recognise my children anywhere.'

He blows me a hug. Two steps back from me he stops and yells, 'Look!' Blowing a hug is sort of like blowing a kiss and he wraps his arms around his body hard and then flings them out into nowhere, everywhere. I feel the force of his action in the subtle touch of the air; I feel the love in the blown hug more than you would feel from a blown kiss.

'We don't have to touch,' he says.

''Cause you're always getting nits,' I lie.

'Because I don't want to always hug,' he says more honestly. 'Only sometimes, Mummy, when I really need to.' And he does – every few days we hug for real, long and hard and say how much we love each other.

A hug every two or three days isn't enough. You must try to make it part of his routine. Make it a natural social behavior.

'Who?' I demand to know. 'Who doesn't think it's enough?' I sit rigid in my chair whose design means you have to unnaturally recline in order to look out of the window. It's not like I don't try, I think.

The world doesn't think it's enough.

Later on, with Marlow, I'll make light of the whole thing and we'll do Pierce Brosnan impressions: The world doesn't think it's enough – the world is not enough. And the conversation and bitter coffee will bite at my throat.

The other mothers have babies in their arms and their elder children clinging to them. I smile as Felix counts the families. 'Francis's family is six, and Jack's got four others, we are a family of two – we were once three but then Daddy went, but that's okay because he's still my family just not our family. Today we are two.' We start walking home together.

'What colour is Francis's hair?' I ask.

He looks confused for a moment. 'I can't recall.'

He's not affectionate enough. His teachers say it took him six months to recognise and name his classmates …

Marlow bursts through the door. Felix rushes at her and stops on the black tile and starts talking continually: 'Remember that day when we walked to the park and I fell over on the footpath and you smacked the cement with your rolled-up newspaper and said, "Naughty footpath for hurting Felix"?'

Marlow kisses the top of his head. 'Sure do, Kiddo.' She mouths silently to me, *I can't believe he remembers that – what was he, two?*

'Hey, Marlow,' Felix is tapping her arm, 'have you ever noticed how a dog can understand a human, but a human can't understand a dog?'

Marlow winks at me. 'You have one switched-on kid.'

It's not bad parenting – you can't blame yourself for this. Not everyone is going to understand, so get tough… You'll learn to recognise true support.

I smile proudly, beam actually, and then frown. 'You're breaking my heart, Marlow. Anyway, he probably got it from a movie.'

'So, he'll be one of those weird people who quote things.'

'They say one more incident and they'll suspend him again.'

A male friend of mine defends Felix and I find myself softening, weakening, every time he does so. I wish sometimes he'd stop. The next time we speak I'm mean to him. It's subtle, and he thinks I'm in a bad mood. He looks hurt momentarily, recovers, and shakes his head. I think he wonders why he bothers.

You should think long and hard about having any more children – your family history – the likelihood of having another …

We are sitting outside in the barbecue area and Marlow is stretching out just shy of the arched shade sail's protection. I stare up from the banana lounge at the soft lemon flecks just visible through the cream and green stripes. I move around, trying to relax as the day warms up, one eye always open and flickering to the sound of Felix's voice.

I watch Marlow reach for her fifth UDL can. I pretend to be too ill to drink today; other days when she isn't looking I take small sips and tip almost all of it in the potted plant nearby.

'You're pushing Tim away,' Marlow analyses.

This conversation is not new.

A ladybird lands on her shoulder and crawls down to the bow of her bikini top; I look away. 'Better now,' I say.

'You need friends.'

'Not friends I want to …'

'Fuck? Marry? Grow old with?' She grins.

'Have babies with,' I say quickly.

'Oh,' she says, 'now you're breaking my heart.'

'Maybe we'll be together in the old people's home. I read this book recently called *Happy Days* – more of a novella really. Maybe we don't have to be that old before we get there.'

She turns slowly and deliberately.

Not wanting another lecture, I talk quickly. 'He's not interested anyhow.'

She looks at me long and hard. She speaks slowly at first, 'I'd say he is.' She pulls at her thumb thoughtfully and the glossy pink of her nail shimmers. 'I'd say he'd pretty much have to be in love with you…considering.' It's my turn to look long and hard.

'Considering what, Marlow?'

She starts to blush red bodily and I remember how my father's skin used to do the same – red hair, pale skin.

I'm afraid to move. I repeat myself, 'Considering what?' My tone is careful now.

'Look, Felix is a good kid.'

I fix my eyes on hers, as if to conquer, all the while praying the cat has made its escape. No such luck. I can see him out of the corner of my eye; cat tucked under one arm, garden shears in the other … somehow climbing. He has that determined look, set mouth against his teeth. The look he reserves for his master plans. I think catapult, but then see the wisp of pink tail hanging from Old Grey's mouth. The cat is huge, but agile. It hunts; it can look after itself. I relax, but only a little. The height and sharpness of the scissor blades has me cautious about startling him. I sit forward.

Marlow is talking fast. 'Face facts, Erin, no one is going to …'

I don't want her to finish. Don't let her finish. I want to be anywhere but here. I get up too quickly and my lounge tips dramatically behind me. I cringe, soften my face and call to Felix to leave Earl alone, get out of the tree and drop the garden shears immediately.

Marlow rises and puts her shirt back on. 'I thought you said the cat's name was Old Grey? Oh, I get it,' she murmurs. 'Yes, funny.'

They say he can't understand social situations – he'll be prone to saying inappropriate things. It runs in families.

He's sitting quietly at the table and I decide it's a good time to ask him to do his homework. It's on measurement – length. The teacher has asked the students to draw around their hands, cut around the outline until they have a paper hand to use to measure objects – like your bed and stuff, I explain to Felix – around the house.

'You get to draw a graph, Felix,' I say cheerfully. Hopefully.

I put all the objects he needs on the coffee table and set the timer on the mantle.

'I could trace around my penis instead … and measure my bed in penises.'

I close my eyes, breathe in and slowly turn. I can hear myself yelling on automatic. He lowers his head and walks to time-out without protest. He doesn't cry, just moves his rock collection to another shelf, makes a Lego windmill, and moves this to the same shelf as the rock collection. It's as if he never said anything.

A clean slate. You must always give him a clean slate.

His father comes to pick him up. He's early for once and I say Felix can only leave after he's cleaned his room.

'It's messy, Felix.'

'It's not messy, it's just …' He grins widely. 'It's just organised chaos.'

My mood lightens, 'Don't *Get Smart* with me.' It's an old joke we've had running for years, handed down by my own mum who is about as funny as me.

My ex-husband buries his head in a cushion to muffle his laughter.

I'm pleased, at least, when I see a hint of a smile on Felix's face. He's starting to understand humour. Once upon a time he only laughed when the jacket of a DVD said 'hilarious,' or 'funniest comedy you'll see all year'. Though, this joke has been explained to him at length.

'I'm sorry, my mummy, for saying things about my penis again.'

I begin to laugh, it's a helpless laugh. I leave the room. I'm worn out.

You're in denial. You have to accept this … even without the label – he's not like everybody else.

Felix is cleaning his room and the phone is ringing in the hall. I know it's Tim and stare intently at the olive receiver, not answering; he doesn't leave a message. My ex-husband is watching me – I can tell, and I finger the fringes of my address book nervously. I know without looking up that his jaw is moving forward – it would be barely noticeable, but it would be moving, involuntarily. Otherwise, he shows no emotion and Felix weaves in, between, and around us.

'Felix, where's your bag of magic tricks?'

Felix runs off to his bedroom and comes back with some cards and three plastic containers. 'I only have two, not a bag-full, Dad. Mum can't afford a bag-full – you know that.'

My ex-husband is chuckling, and I can't help but smile.

'See, Mum. He's fun now he doesn't drink,' says my son.

I look at my ex-husband. He smiles sadly, and then looks ashamed – almost shattered. I've seen Felix's face crumble in the same way … when he hurts his friends or after he tells me he wishes I would die.

'Mummy, why have you stopped laughing?'

You must be tough. Make him make eye contact with you. Don't show his behaviour, life – any of it, is getting to you.

I lock myself in the bathroom and I think about my ex-husband's visits, how he spoils me – gave me a Peter Carey novel, always apologising for before. Not that I can forgive, nor would he want me to – we just lean on each other occasionally in a detached sort of way. I climb into the tub fully clothed and sink into the silky whiteness. I'm still in my jeans and tank top, and the bracelets on my wrists chink against the side. He knocks on the door. 'We'll be going soon.' There's a huge pause. 'Take some time to relax.' I can hear Felix opening the Velcro on his sandals … 'Return your missed call.'

I think of my friend Tim fondly, until his arm coils around my waist and he's here with me, brushing my hair back from my face, lips and breath against my ear. He's a glimmer of something I can't allow. I moan against my own foolishness, and with that I am shivering, and he is gone. I pull my knees to my chest, close my eyes hard against the world, reach for a towel, and stuff it deep inside my mouth.

Bookstore Fetish

Les Zig

Perry drifts through the bookstore, thinking if Elsie's quick, maybe he can get home and catch the second half of the game. Unlikely, though. Elsie's anything but quick. She's treacle. He knows he should be understanding; he should be supportive, the way Elsie's been for him over the last twenty or so years, but for some things his patience wears thin.

He hates bookstores. Doesn't understand the point of them. Or the whole book-buying experience. You read a book, you're done with it. Why would you need to own it? Does the story change on rereading? Why even reread it? Not that Perry ever got as far as reading a book for the first time. Standard fare is comics and sports in the paper, and only over breakfast, or when sitting on the crapper.

Elsie reads. And has forever. In recent years, her volume of reading's grown. Maybe it's because the kids are getting older and need her less. Or maybe it's because they don't do things together like they used to. Not that it would matter if they did. She'd read instead. It's all she does. She reads mornings, before she gets up to start the day. He's sure she reads while he's at work at the garage – she enjoys the soaps, but the feel-good talk shows have never sucked her in. And at night, boy, she reads at night. One time, Perry awoke at 3.00 am, and there she was, still reading, saying she just couldn't put the book down. Perry hollered at her, telling her the book would be there in the morning, and she'd blinked at him, unable to reconcile his rage. It was a damn book. And he needed his sleep. He had work in the morning, after all.

Perry squints at her across the store now, dowdy in her floral dress, swaying like some savant trying to decipher everyday life as she stands in the ROMANCE section searching for her next fix. He snorts, the sort of sound he makes when he wants people to know he's dissatisfied, but there's nobody close enough to hear him. So he snorts again, louder, but still as futilely. Elsie once told him that books offer escapism, but into what? Make-believe? They're just stories.

This had become their ritual. She'd take an hour to find a couple of new books … Well, maybe not an hour. But that's the way it feels. Then, she'd rush up to him like a kid wanting to show off, thrusting her finds into his face, as if these latest discoveries would convert him from his scepticism. Perry never knows what to say. He used to scoff, or try to say something which was meant to be witty but came out stupid. Then her face would shatter. She so wanted him to understand. Even after all this time. Why didn't she just accept he couldn't? Nor did he want to.

Pursing his lips, Perry forces himself through the aisles, looking for diversion, but instead only dismisses books, ignores titles, and disregards covers – unless they offer the titillation of a bit of skin. Then, he'll pause, look around to make sure nobody's watching, pick up the book and flick through it. Just about every time, the cover's a lie, and bears no relationship to the contents.

He rounds the corner and heads into a new aisle, into SCIENCE/RELIGION, but stops, trying to get his bearings as he ponders where SPORTS is. He's been here dozens of times, but the geography never sticks. At least in SPORTS he can amuse himself until Elsie's done. Well, probably. He looks down the aisles, at the signs aligned to the shelves: first NEW AGE, then SELF-HELP, HEALTH, BIO, and then ...

He freezes.

At the opposite end of the store the clerk stands behind the sales counter. Her shape's indistinguishable under a loose blue dress and the bookstore's shapeless knee-length blue apron. She wears a pair of red pumps with low heels, her left foot cocked now upon the ball of the sole, the heel itself elevated daintily above the linoleum floor.

Framed between her red pump and the hem of her apron is the perfect bow of her left calf, her posture pronouncing the firmness of the muscle, the skin unblemished and pale against her outfit.

Perry doesn't move. Doesn't blink. Doesn't breathe.

He's seen calves before. Elsie has two, of course, although they quiver, are prickly with stubble and borderline varicose. It's been three kids and twenty years since Elsie's had the legs of a dancer. But there have been other offerings. Like the long-legged vacuous redhead who comes into the garage to ask the most inane questions about the Beamer her rich parents bought her. She wears minis, or shorts, and exposes a lot more than calf. There's also the girls from the local. Some afternoons, he and the other guys drop in for lunch and – if work's slow – they stay for a show. Those girls reveal even more than the redhead.

Sometimes – particularly after he's had one or two too many – Perry'll slip them a little money, and they'll shake their breasts into his face or gyrate their firm butts onto his lap. Then Perry feels himself respond so painfully that he has to pick at the tent of his overall's crotch to give his erection a bit of freedom.

He knows maybe he should feel guilty about that, like he's cheating on Elsie or something. But nothing's happening. Not really. And like any of those girls would have any real interest in a balding, middle-aged grease monkey with an expanding paunch. If anything, Elsie would be thankful – if she knew – because the nights following these long lunches, he's always in a mood for some loving, and she likes that. She likes him being frisky.

Now, there's none of that.

Nothing but this calf.

What had the clerk looked like? He'd caught a glimpse of her coming in. She was a pretty blonde thing with bobbed hair, pale – the sort who wouldn't tan – and maybe about thirty. Not that he'd really noticed, of course. When you're married, and in accompaniment of said wife, it's never prudent to stare too long (if at all) at other women.

It would be the easiest thing to lift his gaze now, to look at the profile of her face, but instead Perry remains fixed to her left calf. He imagines how smooth it would be under his calloused fingertips, how it would feel against his grizzled face, and how her scent – the mix of whatever perfume she wore and whatever sexual musk she had (as all women had, of that Perry was sure) – would fill his nostrils.

He envisages the swell of her thigh under her dress, the firmness of her leg, and the way her panties – which, Perry visualises as black, lace, and snug – would cup her taut buttocks.

He thinks of the concavity of her waist, how slender it would be, how malleable she would be if he had the arcs of her hips in his hands, and sees the mounds of her breasts, her nipples stiffening in his fingertips and rising like flagpoles upon the bases of her areolae.

He disrobes her of her blue dress and bookstore apron, pulls her panties down her long legs, over her strong thighs, down past those perfect calves, and off her ankles, and lays her before him, savouring the perfection of her body. Her pubic thatch is a small triangle, an arrow pointing him on target. He likes that. He doesn't understand the rage nowadays that less – if not none at all – is better.

Her legs – her calves – rest upon his shoulders, her thighs tensing, and he relishes how tight and hot she is around him as he enters her, his hands locking around her waist, her breasts shimmying as his crotch pounds into her buttocks, an ecstatic hiss of breath escaping her mouth as her upper teeth bite her lower lip.

'Perry?'

It's like a sheaf of paper shearing, and the fantasy is gone, replaced by Elsie standing in front of him, obstructing his view. She holds out a couple of books. Perry doesn't look at the titles, nor their colourful covers. The books are romances – what else are they going to be? He knows that just as he knows that if he looks into Elsie's face, she'll be beaming at him, but wary, afraid he's going to piss all over her love – again.

He forces himself to look at the books. Looks at the titles. At the covers which show some model-perfect buffoon with windswept golden hair holding some swooning dark-haired floozy in his arms. A hundred responses jump into his head. *Real men don't look like that.* Or, *There's nothing fairy tale about love.* And the ever-popular, *Great, now let's get the fuck out of here.*

He looks at her.

Elsie's mouth twitches.

He smiles. 'I think you'll enjoy those.'

Elsie's twitch avalanches her lower lip, causing her mouth to chasm. Her eyes are big round circles, like somebody's taken the ground from beneath her feet and she's falling. But then she forces her mouth closed, and it arches into a grin. Her eyes ignite. The wariness evaporates. She's the woman he fell in love with that first time he saw her, sweet but coy as he caught her eye across the dance floor at one of the clubs he frequented as a teen.

Perry kisses her lightly on the lips, takes her hand in his own, and squeezes it. 'Let's go,' he says.

Together, they go to make her purchases.

Bios

Emilie Collyer is an award-writing playwright and author. Publication credits include *Aurealis*, *The Big Issue*, *Kill Your Darlings*, *Overland*, *Cordite*, *Allegory* (USA), *Dimension6* and two short fiction collections with Clan Destine Press: *A Clean Job* (2013) and *Autopsy of a Comedian* (2015). Emilie's plays are widely produced. Most recently, her sci-fi play *The Good Girl* premiered to sold-out houses and critical acclaim in New York (2016). Website: www.betweenthecracks.net

Patrick Cullen's collection of stories, *What Came Between*, includes five stories published in *The Best Australian Stories*.

Louise D'Arcy has had stories published in many journals and anthologies here and overseas, including *Best Australian Stories 2010, Sleepers Almanac* and *Etchings*. She won the 2010 Age Short Story Award with 'Flat Daddy'. She is an alumnus of Varuna Writers Centre and has been shortlisted for the VarunaHarperCollins Award.

Jane Downing's prose and poetry have been published in Australia and overseas, including in *The Big Issue, Southerly, Westerly, Overland, [untitled], Etchings, Verandah, Visible Ink, Wet Ink, fourW, The Griffith Review, Cordite, The Canberra Times* and *Best Australian Poems 2004* and *2015*. Her two novels (*The Trickster* and *The Lost Tribe*) were published by Pandanus Books.

Erol Engin has lived in Canada, Turkey, and Japan, and now resides in Newcastle, NSW. He currently has a story in *Etchings 11*, and 'The Sea Monkeys' won the 2012 *page seventeen* short story competition.

George Ivanoff is an author and stay-at-home dad residing in Melbourne. He has written more than 90 books for kids and teens, including the *RFDS adventures*, the *You Choose* series and the *Gamers* trilogy. He's had stories and essays in numerous anthologies including *The X-Files: Secret Agendas* (IWD, 2016), *Rich and Rare* (Ford Street Publishing, 2015) and … this one. He's won a few awards including a YABBA and a couple of Chronos Awards. George drinks too much coffee, eats too much chocolate and watches too much Doctor Who. Check out his website: http://georgeivanoff. com.au

Kirk Marshall is an award-winning Australian writer, and teacher of English Literature and Media (Film & TV Studies) at RMIT University. He is the author of *The Signatory* (Skylight Press, 2012); *Carnivalesque, And: Other Stories* (Black Rider Press, 2011); and *A Solution to Economic Depression in Little Tokyo, 1953*. He has written for more than seventy publications, both in Australia and overseas, including *Award Winning Australian Writing, Island, Wet Ink, Going Down Swinging, Voiceworks, Verandah, Visible Ink, fourW, Cordite* and *Mascara Literary Review*. He edits *Red Leaves*, the English-language / Japanese bi-lingual literary journal. He now suffers migraines in two languages.

Ryan O'Neill's latest collection is *Their Brilliant Careers* (Black Inc).

A. S. Patric's debut novel *Black Rock White City* won the 2016 Miles Franklin Award. He is also a winner of the Ned Kelly Award and the Booranga Prize, and is the author of *Las Vegas for Vegans*, a story collection shortlisted in the Queensland Literary Awards. *The Rattler* was shortlisted for the Lord Mayor's Award and his novella, *Bruno Kramzer*, was shortlisted for the Viva La Novella Prize.

Laurie Steed is an author, editor, and reviewer. His fiction has been broadcast on BBC Radio 4 and published in *Best Australian Stories, The Age, Meanjin, Westerly, Island, The Sleepers Almanac* and elsewhere. He won the 2012 Patricia Hackett Prize for Fiction and is the recipient of fellowships and residencies from The University of Iowa, The Baltic Writers Residency, The Sozopol Fiction Seminars, Varuna,

Writers Victoria, The Katharine Susannah Prichard Writers' Centre and The Fellowship of Writers (WA). He lives with his family in Perth, Western Australia.

Blaise van Hecke runs Busybird Publishing with her husband Kev Howlett. Together they pursue all avenues to tell stories and help others tell theirs. A quintessential flower child, Blaise delights in all things magical and is working on too many stories at the same time.

Bel Woods is a Melbourne-based, Tasmanian-born writer. She enjoys both contemporary and lyrical literary fiction, and will often explore female characters and the decisions they do and don't make as a thematic thread. Her writing achievements include publications in *Verity La*, *Vine Leaves*, *The Victorian Writer* and *Westerly*, among others.

Les Zig has had stories and articles published in various journals, and also had three screenplays optioned. His website and blog can be found at http://www.leszig.com/

Credits

'The Artist, At Frankston and Lowe', was published first in *dotdotdash* magazine (Perth, 2009) and later in Kirk's fiction debut, *Carnivalesque, And: Other Stories* (Black Rider Press, 2011).

'Bookstore Fetish' was published in *Wet Ink 21* (2010).

'The Eleventh Summer' was placed second in the Society of Women Writers' (Vic) 2007 biennial short story competition and published in the anthology *Mud Puddles* in 2008.

'Flat Daddy' won the 2010 Age Short Story Award and was published in *The Age* January 2010 and in *Award Winning Stories*.

'A History of the Kenny Gang' was published in *Visible Ink 23* (2011).

'How My Father Dies at the End' was published in *New Australian Stories 2* (Scribe 2010). Ash and Destiny enjoy

Ash and Destiny enjoy a happy life in Melbourne with their young son, Tomas, a large and slightly dysfunctional family, a successful art gallery, and Destiny's new exhibition about to debut. But everything changes for Ash on one extremely hot Summer Solstice when a car crash leaves his family shattered.

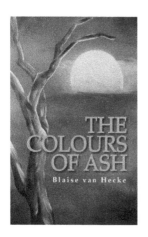

Waking in hospital Ash knows his whole life has been flipped on its head and his long journey to adjusting to loss and pain is just about to begin. But as time passes both Ash and Destiny struggle to return to their normal life in Melbourne.

When all seems to be lost and stagnating in their lives, the option to move to country Victoria presents itself. An unlikely move for the city-dwelling couple turns into a new and rejuvenating experience that is the start of a new family, connection to old family, and a healing process for all, despite more disasters looming in the distance

Luke Miggs wants more than small-town life: the grind of chores on the family farm, playing footy, and drinks with friends. Like maybe doing something about his crush on Amanda Hunt, a barmaid at the local pub who's smart, funny, and ambitious. Or playing footy in the big league. At eighteen, it can't be too late, can it?

When Adam Pride emerges from the night and tells the Ravens he wants to play for them, everything begins to change. But with that change comes a mystery – who is Adam, and what is his link to Claude Rankin, the tyrannical captain-coach of the reigning champions?

Pride is a story of friendship, bonds, and coming of age, and how the choices of our past can come back to shape our future.

www.ingramcontent.com/pod-product-compliance
Ingram Content Group Australia Pty Ltd
76 Discovery Rd, Dandenong South VIC 3175, AU
AUHW021838190325
408583AU00009B/55

9 780995 350328